Savannah

Time

www.cyberworldpublishing.com

ISBN 978-1-921879-63-0

All characters in this book are the product of the author's imagination and no
resemblance to real people, or implication of events occurring in actual places,
is intended.

Cyberworld Publishing
Jindalee St
Toronto, Australia

Books By Olivia Stowe

Charlotte Diamond Mysteries
By the Howling
Retired With Prejudice
Coast to Coast
An Inconvenient Death

Savannah Series
Chatham Square
Savannah Time

Other books
Fiddler's Rest
Spirit of Christmas

Savannah

Time

Olivia Stowe

Sequel to

Chatham Square

Chapter One

"It's hardly noticeable now."

"Yes, she's almost worked it into her regular gait to make it charming," Ginny responded. "She has taken adversity and turned it into a strength—just as all of us knew she would. That's what made what we contributed worthwhile. Everything about Samantha is charming. She's grown up into quite a lovely young woman."

"Yes she has. We have every right to be proud of our young Ms. Johnson."

The two were standing at the parlor window of Rose Drayton's ochre stuccoed Gothic Revival mansion on the east side of Savannah's Chatham Square. They were looking out at the couple that had come together at a bench—what the two women liked to smile and refer to as Rose's bench—out at the center of the square. The young man had just approached the bench, where the young woman had been sitting, looking pensively, not seeming to notice the beauty of the park around her—certainly not exhibiting that she expected to meet there with the young man.

This was the showiest time of the year for this Savannah square, part of the original twenty-four-square plan designed for the city in the mid eighteenth century. But now Chatham Square was one of the most remote and quiet of the twenty-one oases of tranquility that survived the brief march of progress the historical city was subjected to in the mid nineteenth century. The graceful live oaks forming a canopy overhead, with their lacy dripping icings of Spanish moss, were as they ever had been. Underneath them, however, spread in the beds separated by the wide, bricked walkways winding across the square in all directions, were mature azalea and rhododendron bushes that were in full bloom in early spring, providing a riot of color that would fade into wilted green-upon-green aspect under the heat and humidity that inevitably would creep into the southern coastal city before spring was half spent. Even in winter the live oaks and the azaleas and rhododendrons would retain their leaves, and only a rare dusting of snow and the change in apparel of those walking its pathways would betray the park's state of dormancy. Other than the subtle changes of seasons, the square—and the historical district of Savannah that embraced it—offered a suspension of years, reflecting the ambience of the old South. Its movement through time was glacial, with only the occasional intrusion of an automobile on the streets bordering the square giving a clue to what century it was in—or that time was passing at all. Ginny liked to think of this seeming suspension in time as "Savannah time."

The young woman, her smooth chocolate-brown skin set off by the white cotton linen summer frock that flowed down her trim body in model-proud folds, had just reached the bench and sat down. She had a knitting bag with her, and Ginny knew that the young woman would be using the spare moments between checking on Edward James over at the Pitt Bookstore at the southwest corner of the square and fixing Arnie Richard's lunch working on the tartan for the Scottish doll. Ginny was the art doll maker and Samantha was her quite able assistant—as well as assisting others on the square in so many ways.

Ginny didn't even try to deny the young woman had an ability to make dolls come alive that would be able, with time and practice, to surpass even her own. There were so few young people picking up the handicraft that Ginny taught at the Savannah College of Arts and Design—SCAD to the locals— and few of those had the natural talent for it that Samantha had. It was this knowledge that conflicted Ginny so on what she should encourage Samantha to do at this important crossroad of her life—and how much of whatever she counseled was because of what she, Ginny, wanted.

"Never a wasted moment," Ginny thought. "And moving in a seamless flow from one task to another." These thoughts should have pleased Ginny, but they made her sigh instead. Samantha was nearly eighteen. As painful as it would be for everyone, it was time for the young lady to step out of that flow of tasks. The time was at hand—if it ever was to be.

As they watched, a young white man, all legs and gangling stride, had appeared from the north side of the square from the direction of the Barnard building of SCAD, zeroed in on the bench when he saw Samantha sitting there, and now stood beside where she sat and leaned over to speak to her. He was carrying several bulky grocery bags, one of which he placed on the bench by Samantha's side.

Rose chuckled, and Ginny turned to look at her. She was pleased to see that the wrinkles on the old woman's face still held their laugh lines. The laugh lines didn't detract from the perfect bone structure of her face that made her beauty— despite the strain of the last two years—ageless. Not for the first time, in memory of the Rose she had first met, Ginny found herself surfacing the phrase, "She cleans up real good."

After all that Rose had been through in the last couple of years with Clayton's illness, it was good to see that the woman hadn't lost her mental edge and sense of humor. But sadly, Ginny had to acknowledge that Rose wasn't, in fact, as sharp now as she had been a few years ago. Ginny had never deciphered how old the woman was—and Rose certainly wasn't telling. Rose was the secretive type, something that Ginny had first experienced a decade earlier when she'd taken the woman for a homeless bag lady defending her "queen of the square" possession of that bench Samantha was sitting on. Ginny was eventually to find out—not because Rose told her— that Rose's family was prominent in Savannah and that she owned this mansion as well as the Armstrong Inn on the south side of the square and several nightclubs across Georgia and down to New Orleans itself—and that, in all likelihood, Rose paid for that bench out in the square too.

"What do you find amusing?" Ginny asked.

"Those two, out there on the square. Him mooning over her and her pretending she doesn't notice. Remembering them out there ten years ago. Can you?"

"Ah, yes. Jeff Turnball was just another young ruffian of the square then, wasn't he? As I remember, he and another boy teased Samantha mercifully because of her crippled leg and because she couldn't keep up with them."

"And how that worm has turned now, hasn't it? Samantha's leg has been improved, and she's now perfection itself. And now the Turnball boy sees her for what she always was."

"Yes, but Jeff grew up too. He's quite a thoughtful young man now. He'll be over here with your groceries when Samantha shoos him away."

"Yes, he's quite a godsend. I don't know what Clayton and I would do without him. I certainly can't find the time to be away to do any grocery shopping." Rose sighed.

"I'm sorry I didn't get to visit with Clayton today—and that I haven't found time to come here more often."

"I regret he'll have missed your visit too. But he'd just managed to get to sleep—and he had such a rough night." She sighed again.

"Has the pain gotten worse for him?"

"It's hard to tell. He's so stoic about it. You know Clayton. And he won't let them increase the medication. He says it confuses him. And when he's able, he's furiously scribbling away. I'm sure there's one more poetry book in him. But he won't let me read any of it."

"I'll bet that's because it's all about you—and I'll also bet it will be one of his best." Ginny changed the subject, though, seeing that Rose had blushed. "I could stay with him for awhile now if you wished to go out and do some shopping."

"No, thank you, Ginny. That's kind of you. But I think I'll stay put with him. One never knows when that last opportunity of contact will come. And the two of us missed out on so many opportunities earlier in life."

"I know, Rose. But you're together now."

"Not completely. Not even now."

Ginny winced at that—and not just because her two elderly friends still weren't married, having found each other at last, after years of misunderstanding and misplaced resentment on Clayton's part, but also because Ginny herself wasn't completely divorced from a very similar predicament. It had been a misunderstanding that had severed her from her own "significant other," Lenny Taylor. While he was serving abroad in the Near East wars, Lenny had been victimized by an army buddy who led him to believe that Ginny had been unfaithful to him and who had gone to the lengths of sending Ginny a nasty "Dear Jane" letter on Lenny's behalf but without Lenny's knowledge. Lenny and Ginny had both been teaching at Virginia Commonwealth University in Richmond—she textile design and he graphics arts—when Lenny was sent away with the National Guard. The false, but nasty, break in their relations had sent Ginny in retreat to Savannah to the Chatham Square apartment she inherited from an aunt and a teaching position at SCAD.

Lenny had returned from Iraq and, having found out how the other soldier had destroyed their relationship, had sought out Ginny in Savannah. They made up, and Lenny transferred his teaching position to SCAD. But they hadn't married and there continued to be a slight strain of trust in their relationship. Two years ago Lenny had gone back to VCU and Richmond on what was supposed to be a temporary teaching assignment—but two years had gone by now and he and Ginny were still apart and in limbo.

The story of Rose Drayton and Clayton Winthrop was both more romantic and much more tragic, but the effect had been the same. Rose and Clayton had grown up on Chatham Square, across the park from each other. They and Stephen Dupree, each studying in different areas of the arts—Rose in voice, Clayton in poetry, and Stephen in fine arts—had been inseparable in college. The romance had been between Rose and Clayton, and Stephen had stood by loyally as Clayton's best friend. Clayton had been drafted and sent to Vietnam, where he was falsely reported to have been killed. Mutual mourning of the loss of Clayton had thrown Rose and Stephen together. This had led to their marriage.

When Clayton returned from Vietnam, not knowing until years later that he'd been declared dead, all he saw was his best friend married to his own intended. Rose could have told him about the false death notice then, but by then Stephen was dying and she couldn't leave him—the situation had not been his fault in any way. Rose felt it was her fault. She had withdrawn into a world of recluse and near insanity, and she and Clayton had continued living across Chatham square from each other for decades without contact, Clayton eaten with resentment and Rose with regret.

Ginny had forced the two of them to see what had happened to them and to realize that it had been no one's fault. It had been mutual love for the presumed lost Clayton that had brought Rose and Stephen together. Rose and Clayton had become reconciled enough that Clayton had moved to Rose's house a bit more than a half decade previously. But they had never married. And now Clayton, like Stephen before him, was slowly dying, and Rose, not in much better health herself, was determined to stick with him to the end.

In the intervening years, Clayton, an internationally renowned poet, had kept his fine old Savannah townhouse across Chatham Square from Rose's house in good repair, but unoccupied. It existed as a visual symbol that Rose and Clayton were not really completely "together."

It was Clayton's unoccupied house that drew Ginny's attention again as she stood at the window of Rose's manse and looked out over Chatham Square.

"There's a moving van in front of Clayton's house," Ginny said, the surprise showing in her voice.

"Yes, yes, there is."

"He hasn't—?"

"Sold? No. But it's been vacant so long. A writer friend of his wants to spend a year in Savannah working on her next novel of the South, and Clayton saw no reason not to let her live there."

"Anyone I might know?"

"Helena Jordan. Do you know of her?"

"The former movie actress? The one who writes those rather bitchy romances about movie stars out in Hollywood?"

"I suppose so. I haven't read anything by her myself." Something in the way Rose said that made Ginny turn and look at her. It was as if there was something about the other woman that Rose didn't like.

"That doesn't surprise me. A novel set in the South—in Savannah? That's hardly her style. Where does she know Clayton from?"

"I'm not really sure. He was rather vague on that point himself. I think she contacted him. He said she seemed rather insistent—both about their literary connections and her wish to rent his house for a year. I don't—"

Rose didn't end that thought because an anguished sound of pain rolled down the hall from the study behind the parlor. The study had been converted to Clayton's bedroom so that he didn't have to try to negotiate stairs.

"I'm coming, Clayton," Rose called out immediately. She turned away from the window.

"He sounds like he's in great pain—and upset," Ginny murmured, as she too turned away from the window.

15

"It's often like this—now—when he awakes, having slept through a scheduled medication. He will be ill-tempered for a while—but we'll soon see to that."

"I'd best leave then without visiting him," Ginny said.

"Yes, thank you for understanding. I think that would be best. He'd be embarrassed to know that you have been here when he is at his rawest. You know how well he thinks of you; he wants you to think of him as he once was. I'll call you later when his medications have taken hold, if you like, and you can come back and see him then."

"Yes, thanks. I'll keep my cell phone open. But if it's not convenient today, just don't worry about calling."

"You're an angel, Ginny," Rose said, as they both crossed the room, Rose toward the study and Ginny toward the front foyer. "Always have been."

"I think you're the one proving to be the square's angel, Rose."

"If you don't count Samantha," Rose answered. And then she laughed and set her face in a smile to offer Clayton when she reached his bedside.

Descending Rose's front porch stairs and walking along the eastern side of Chatham Square toward the converted townhouse on the south side where her own second-story apartment was located, Ginny was hailed from William's Café on the same side of the square as Rose's house.

"Come sit with me, love. I'll let you treat me to this cappuccino."

"Oh, hi, Tony. I haven't seen you for a few days. I'd be happy to let you buy *me* a latte," she said with a sweet smile.

Ginny could see that the resident of the basement of her townhouse was dressed as flamboyantly as ever and had that same pursed-lip mischievous smirk on his face as usual as she moved past two women sitting at a table near the entrance to the café's outdoor section and joined Tony at his table.

"Busman's holiday?" Ginny asked, as she sat down. A waiter was there immediately, and Ginny asked for a latte. She didn't ask for any of the fancy, pricier versions they served here, though, as she knew the café would provide the drink to her gratis because she was sitting with Tony. Both she and Tony knew he'd been joking about her treating him to a drink.

"I don't work here much anymore," Tony answered. "Much too busy down at Club One. I'm the manager there now, you know. It takes up simply too much of my time. I still performing too—they didn't want me to stop doing that."

"I can imagine so, your Marie Antoinette must still be their big draw."

They both laughed. "Why, I should certainly hope so, sugar," Tony answered, the androgynous coffee-and-cream laugh lines under his high cheek bones creasing charmingly.

When Ginny had originally met Tony—her first friend on Chatham Square—he had been the head waiter at this café. He also performed at one of the premier transvestite clubs in downtown Savannah, and now his work with the club was taking over his life. He had been accepted so well in the social group that had formed on the square—primarily around a

17

mutual community interest in helping Samantha Johnson receive the surgical attention she needed to improve her leg deformity—that, as his finances improved from the heightened profile of his performance art, he had moved onto the square himself.

"I see you've been at Rose and Clayton's," he said.

"Yes."

"And how did you find Clayton?"

"Asleep, resting—which apparently is most comfortable for him now." Ginny knew she could have told Tony that she hadn't been able to visit with Clayton because he had awakened in pain and ill spirits, but she saw no reason to pick at the concern they all felt.

"And Rose?"

"A bit frazzled."

"How long do you think she'll be able to cope?"

"I don't know. And I'm sure she's avoiding thinking about it. I'm sure you know how wrenching it would be for her to have to leave the square—for them to go into a home."

"But that's rather inevitable, isn't it?" Tony asked. His voice was soft, which was unusual for him. He was usually pleasantly braying and being as naughty and off color as he thought he could get away with. Ginny didn't think it was just the subject that had him subdued. The presence of the two women at the other table—both smartly dressed and looking a bit haughty, one rather possessively hanging on to the other—was making them both reserved and speaking in low tones. The women were intently staring out onto the square, though,

18

and Ginny was sure they weren't following her conversation with Tony, even if they could hear smatterings of it.

"Yes, I suppose it is—especially as long as Samantha is still around to help them out. Without Samantha, I'm afraid they couldn't hack it."

"Ah, Samantha, sweet Samantha. What are we going to do about Samantha?"

Ginny didn't answer. She didn't have an answer. But she also didn't have to ask Tony what he meant.

* * * *

"Come on, Sam, you know you'd enjoy it." Jeff Turnball was standing over Samantha, one foot up on the bench seat, at the opposite end of the bench that Samantha was sitting on, trying not to be threateningly close to her. But he was such a tall, gangling figure that it was hard not getting the impression that he was looming over her. And it was equally clear that he was mooning for her—that he'd like nothing so much as to take her in his arms and hug her close.

"Is there anything perishable in those grocery bags?" Samantha asked, her voice clear and spine tingling with the lushness of her southern drawl. "If Rose gets her quart of cherry vanilla ice cream half melted, there will be the devil to pay."

"No, nothing that will spoil or melt. All dry goods. We can sit out here and chat all day."

"No we can't. I have to go over and fix Arnie his lunch in a couple of minutes. And I'm sure you are cutting it close on basketball practice or something. Besides, I'm the only one sitting, it seems—which is probably right. You need to get those groceries delivered, so you need to get those big feet of yours moving."

Jeff let the "big feet" comment go by, but he shuddered inside, connecting it with how he used to make fun of Samantha's crippled leg. He'd been nearly five years trying to make that go away—something he knew he never could fully erase—ever since Samantha had started to blossom into a lovely young woman and he realized he loved her. "You're changing the subject, Ms. Johnson. You can't be the square's Florence Nightingale day in and day out. There's a party on at SCAD Saturday night, and I know you'll want to go to that. We could go listen to your dad's first set at the Jazz'd Tapa Bar earlier. You'll enjoy it. And you need the change."

He'd called it a party that was on at SCAD, not a dance. He knew that, no matter how much better Samantha's leg was after the series of surgeries she'd undergone nearly ten years previously, there was no dancing in her future. It was just one of the topics he walked on egg shells about in his attempt to woo the young beauty.

Samantha wasn't shy about bringing up another sticking point.

"You know that wouldn't be right. Jeff. This is Savannah we live in. I know it's being done most everywhere now, but this is Savannah—we're still in the South and, in many ways, still in the last century. I'm sure your father wouldn't—"

"My father is just fine with it, Sam. He's the one who's gotten after me to ask you out."

This was true. Jeff's father, with whom he'd lived in a basement apartment on the square since as long as Jeff could remember, had flatly told Jeff to stop obsessing over Samantha Johnson or what anyone thought of seeing the two of them together and to get out there and court her. People had never been able to gauge his father well. He was a reserved and gruff man who managed the grocery store that Jeff was delivering for. He'd come to Savannah with his toddler son and no wife years ago and hadn't said a thing to satisfy the gossip concerning where Jeff's mother was and why they'd come to Savannah. As punishment for that, he was written off as a disagreeable redneck and rough character who was scrupulously honest and helpful at the grocery store, but who rarely smiled and was best avoided.

But that wasn't the father Jeff knew. To him, his father was sensitive and would do whatever he needed to do to make life better for his son—and for anyone else who asked. And as for Samantha and Savannah, Jeff knew without a doubt that his father was colorblind, that he took people as they came and in terms of how they acted—that white or black didn't matter to him a bit. There hadn't been a hint of color bar when he'd told Jeff to get off his tail mooning over Samantha and to get out there and win her.

Samantha sighed. "As it happens, I'll be going to the SCAD party. I've already been asked."

"Bill Madison?"

"Yes, William's asked me."

Jeff involuntarily lifted his gaze to the south side of the square, to a brownstone townhouse located half way between the one where he and his dad lived in the basement and the one where Samantha's family lived on the third floor. No apartment for William Madison, though, Jeff thought bitterly. The Madisons were among the black elite in Savannah—having been in business here since Reconstruction, and not letting anyone forget that. And Mr. Madison was some sort of important lawyer. The family's status was symbolized no better than in Madison's insistence to be called "William" rather than the less-pretentious "Bill." Not that Jeff would stop calling him Bill, if only so he could enjoy the reaction he got when he did so to the young man's face.

William Madison was the same age as Jeff, but whereas Jeff had taken two years off between high school and college to earn enough money to start college, Madison had gone straight into SCAD as an architecture student. Madison was stuffy and snobbish. Jeff couldn't fathom what William Madison had to offer to Samantha other than money and a good upper-middle-class family name in Madison. But then Jeff was afraid he did know. Madison was black and Jeff wasn't.

"If I'd asked you first, would you have gone with me instead? I mean, I can always look far ahead and ask you to something else now, if that's—"

22

"Jeff, don't," Samantha said. "You're going away for college. I know that's your dream. To go into hotel management—for that degree you've got to go away. I'll be here in Savannah. It just wouldn't—"

"I'll be coming back. You know my ambition is to work at the Armstrong Inn—right here on the square. And, besides, you need to go away to college too, Sam. I know you want to be a doctor. You can't study to do that and stay here on Chatham Square. You need to get away too—if at least for a couple of years."

"There's so much here needing done. So many who need me to help with—"

"That's no sort of life, Sam, doing for everyone else but yourself. You need to live too. You need to live before you die."

Samantha stood up from the bench, punctuating the end to this particular conversation—one that she'd had with Jeff before. One she'd had with her own parents. One she wanted to stop having. She was sorry she'd ever told anyone she wanted to be a doctor. It just complicated everything and brought up concerns. She didn't want to be the center of concern. It had been a wonderful thing how the people of the square had come together to help get her the surgeries needed to help her walk better—and without the perpetual pain she'd grown up with—but many was the time that she wished they hadn't done it, that they hadn't focused on her. She wanted just to stand in the shadows and not be a concern or burden for anyone else. And she felt eternally beholden to these people now. Many of them needed her now. Rose and Clayton, trying

23

to live out their lives in their beloved square; Arnie Richards, her downstairs neighbor and super, who no longer could walk out of his own building. Even Ginny Standler, who increasingly relied on Samantha for her demanding doll making business.

The Madisons—William and his parents—were a solid, undemanding fixture on the square. But even they were set too high for her. Her origins were too humble—daughter of a hotel maid and a jazz trumpeter. She didn't, truthfully, see a future with William. But letting it lie out there was a good counterbalance for what she knew wasn't possible with Jeff Turnball.

She just wanted everything to go on as it was. She didn't want to be graduating from high school. She didn't want to face any of the decisions pressing at her.

"It's time for Arnie's lunch. I have to go in now, Jeff."

"Sam." It was almost a plaintive wail of a sound. But Samantha had already stood and started to stride off, toward the converted apartment building her family shared with Arnie Richards, Ginny Standler, and Tony on the south side of Chatham Square. Retreating into the safety of the life she had established for herself, working on fulfilling the needs of those around her. Trying to fulfill their expectations as well was just too much for her to face.

Besides, where would the money come from for her to go to the university, followed by medical school? A fortune had already been spent on her surgeries—more, she strongly suspected, than either she or her parents had ever been told. And she felt like she could never repay the people who came

24

together to make those possible. What right did she have to any more financial backing? It didn't require any schooling at all for her to play nurse to the needs of her friends here on the square.

* * * *

"Isn't he a bit young for you?"

"Let's not be catty, Jane." The woman sat back in her chair at the outside table at William's Café, adjusted her cashmere shawl on her bare shoulders, and blew a smoke ring at her table companion. "I was just watching the movers manhandle your baby grand up the stairs of the house, hoping perhaps that they would drop it and smash it into a thousand pieces so I didn't have to listen to your maudlin version of 'The Moonlight Sonata' ever again."

"Now you're the one being catty, Helena. And I could have sworn your eyes were on that handsome young man hovering over the black girl on the bench out in the middle of the square. He is quite a fine-looking young man, I'll admit. But you're old enough to be his mother . . . at least."

The romantic novelist Helena Jordan blew another smoke ring and put her cigarette down in the ash tray long enough to take a swig from her glass of chardonnay. It was a glorious afternoon sitting beside Chatham Square with its magnificent tree cover and lush lawn. The azaleas were absolutely gorgeous. She was glad they'd arrived before those

25

faded. She already was feeling that this was the right decision to come here. It was time. She had put it off for so long.

She also couldn't resist teasing Jane a bit. Jane was so insecure about their relationship.

"Yes, he does cut a fine figure, doesn't he?" Helena let out a sigh. "I can tell that this will be the perfect setting for a new novel. It will practically write itself."

"But so tear jerky. A woman trying to capture a past that she has given up to pursue a successful career. Finding out that it wasn't the type of success that fulfilled her. It's been done a million times, Helena. I keep telling you that. You want to talk about maudlin . . . and Savannah. Who wants to read about a backwater like Savannah. They'll compare it to *Gone with the Wind*. Can you even write Southern? Your genre is the catty tinsel town of Hollywood."

"Maudlin sells, Jane. And if they compare it with *Gone with the Wind*, who cares as long as they say I'm a better writer than Margaret Mitchell was? When they think of that work, they think of the Hollywood movie, anyway. That sort of drama is right up my line. I've told you before. You didn't have to come out here with me. I could have done this alone. You can go back to L.A. if this will be too trying for you. And, besides, I think it's a story I can tell with feeling."

She had spoken harshly—more harshly than she had intended. But Jane had cut too close to the quick with her remarks. Helena felt that she was losing her grip on the writing. There were no new scenarios coming to her mind. She had needed a jolt, a change in scenery and setting. And, besides, she never would reveal to Jane Seldon that she hadn't really come here to write a book. Or that there was every reason why she should know how to write "Southern."

Jane went white and turned to the only occupied table in the café to see if the thirtyish but fashionable enough raven-haired woman sitting incongruously with the garishly obvious black man of almost indeterminate gender had heard Helena castigate her. There was no evidence she had. The two of them seemed to be in a very intense conversation themselves, which was quite a change in the black man since the woman had arrived at the café. He'd been flippant with the waiter before that in a way that Jane felt was downright disrespectful. Diners were not that familiar with the help in L.A.

"I'm sorry, Jane. I didn't mean to bite your head off. It's just that I'm so tired with this moving and all of these decisions that have nothing to do with my writing."

Jane Seldon was sniffling, but she gave the novelist—the woman who controlled the purse strings and every facet of her life now—a little fluttering-eyelashes smile. Above all else she needed to maintain her hold on Helena Jordan. The novelist had been acting so strange of late, and this move to Savannah, even if temporary, was completely out of character. Jane sensed that there was something running beneath the surface of Helena Jordan that was new and intense and insistent—and quite possibly threatening to their relationship. Was there another woman? Or, worse, another man? Here in Savannah? Was that the real reason they had been uprooted from their normal existence and had been carted out to this sleepy backwater?

And she didn't like at all the way Helena had been looking at that young man at the bench out in the middle of the square. Watching the piano being lifted up the steps to their rented house across the square? Fat chance of that. She had been scrutinizing the young man. But Helena had always been changeable. Never fully satisfied with anything. Jane had managed to handle that before. She would handle it now as well.

Chapter Two

"Have you given any thought to telling her?"

"You know the terms of the bequest, Ginny," Rose responded. "She isn't to know about it until she's eighteen. She has several more months before that."

The two of them were sitting out in the middle of the square, on the center bench—Rose's bench—as they had been doing for a decade, ever since Rose permitted Ginny to cross the path from the other bench and share this one with her. That had marked the beginning of a long, close friendship.

They were out here this Saturday morning not to just to soak up the divine weather—although they certainly were doing that—but primarily because Clayton didn't want Rose in the house for a while. Rose had gotten too feeble to move him around for his sponge bath herself—in truth, he'd never let her bathe him—but he would let Samantha do it. And he didn't want Rose in the house while that was going on. Rose didn't object, as it was one of the few periods of time she could be out of the house without feeling guilty about it. But she did feel guilty about what Samantha had to do.

"We weren't thinking straight when we set that condition," Ginny answered. "We meant it for her college fund, and eighteen is too late for her to find out that she has enough money to go to college for at least a couple of years. If she doesn't know about it until she's eighteen, it will set her back at least a semester, or maybe even more. And the longer Samantha puts off going to college, the less likely she'll wind up do it."

Rose didn't say anything. She just plucked a piece of material from her bag; moved it this way and that, taking a close look at it; and, eventually, whacked away at it with a heavy pair of fabric scissors.

Ginny looked away and smiled. There had been a time—during what several called Rose's "bag lady days"— when Ginny saw this behavior as a sign that Rose was demented and when Ginny even was a bit afraid for her own physical safety. But that all changed the day she went into her guestroom to discover a cleverly pieced, gaily colored patchwork quilt that Rose had made for her. This close examination followed by butchering of pieces of material was just Rose's way of envisioning what inevitably turned out to be a marvelously artistic quilt.

When Rose didn't say anything, Ginny did. She hadn't wanted to say anything at all, but someone needed to force some movement here. "Everyone is still here who put the fund

30

together over the last decade. We could just all agree to tell her now. There's no one to complain if we all agree to it."

Rose set her face in a determined mold. The piece of cloth she was holding was a problem, obviously. It was possible that it couldn't find a place in the quilt she was working on at all. And it seemed that this conundrum required her full attention. But this time she did speak . . . eventually.

"Do you think that I don't want her to go to college? That I am so selfish I don't want anything to change? For her to go?"

"Oh, Rose, honey. No I don't think that—at least no more than I am thinking it. I know you want only the best for Samantha. But it is all going to change anyway . . . isn't it? I don't want to lose her either. It's not just that she saves time and increases doll production, but that the work she does inspires me. I can't imagine that I will be as creative as this myself when Samantha is gone. But it's going to change anyway. I don't want it to, but sometimes I have a lucid moment and accept that it will. I'm sorry, but how much longer do you think you and Clayton can hold out here even with Samantha's help? And Arnie. I'm surprised he's still with us. And I'm even more surprised about Edward. Samantha's even helping with him. She's a natural healer. You know as well as I do that her dream has long been to become a doctor. It's only in recent years that she's stopped saying that. And that she stopped saying that should have been a signal to us, don't you think?"

"Seems to me that you are giving reasons why Samantha should stay—to hold us all together as long as possible." Rose sighed then, hovered her scissors over the

31

scrap of cloth she was holding and then, with a shrug, whacked away at it with determined, precise strokes. "But you are right, of course, that Samantha won't hold back time for us either."

It had surprised Ginny a bit that she had included Tom Thornton's companion, Edward James, in her litany of those Samantha was ministering too—although of course, now that she thought about it, Samantha spent a significant amount of time at the Pitt Bookstore catty-corner from the southwest corner of the square. Tom Thornton managed the store, and his live in, Edward James, was a big reason why Ginny had come to Savannah. She had taken his position at SCAD when he'd gone off on a temporary posting. He had been ill, and thought he was dying before he left. He had taken the assignment because he didn't want to burden Tom with a terminal illness. Ginny had urged Tom to go to him, despite Edward's stated wish, which he did. And when Edward didn't die, they both returned to Savannah. Edward hadn't died from his heart condition now for ten years.

"Perhaps I should consult with Samantha's father about it."

"That might be a good idea, yes," Ginny answered. She could see that Rose was tearing up, and Ginny, afraid she'd already pushed her too far, didn't want to push Rose any harder on this. After all, nearly all of the money in the college fund the circle of friends on the square had put together for Samantha without her knowledge was either Rose's or Clayton's.

"Yes, that's what I'll do," Rose said, in a voice of determination. "When it seems appropriate."

Ginny watched as Rose decided that the new piece of cloth she was fingering would work in her quilt and began brutally reshaping and sizing it with her shears.

* * * *

"Have you run out of reading material already, Ginny? Didn't I sell you one of those Venice detective stories just last week? Finished it already?"

"No, I'm still reading it. And, as always, your recommendation was impeccable, Tom. I'm actually here to see Edward. Is he upstairs in the apartment?"

"No," the manager of the Pitt Bookstore answered. "This was a good day for him. He's gone over to Barnard Hall."

"Ah, good, I'll catch him over at SCAD then. I need to go over my course content with him for next semester. He's had such great ideas since you two came back and he took the departmental chair position. I feel like there's something missing in my textiles course, and he's perhaps the world's leading expert on that. But I'm glad he's gone over to Barnard Hall. It's a sign that he's feeling chipper."

"Yes, that's a miracle—that he is feeling so well." Then Tom's voice took on a more somber tone. "Then you're planning to be here another semester? If you're already setting up your curriculum for it."

Ginny looked sharply at Tom, slouched behind his desk and looking rather pale. She'd noticed that he'd been looking pretty worn around the edges for some time, but for some reason he looked unusually pale today. Ginny cared about Tom. She had once even thought he might be the one for her—after her relationship with Lenny had initially gone on the rocks. Tom was quite nice looking and he was a gentle, kind man, with a sensitive nature and a good sense of humor. It had taken a strong hint from Rose to wise Ginny up to Tom's natural inclination. But that hadn't stopped her from caring about him.

"Why, yes. Yes I am." It was an answer, but it was more a question, and Tom knew that it was.

"Here, sit," he said, and he moved a stack of books at the edge of the desk so that Ginny could perch there. He had chairs scattered around because the bookstore's policy was to encourage browsing, but he knew that Ginny preferred to perch. "How long has it been since Lenny has been back at VCU?"

"Oh, I don't know."

"I do. Almost two years. As sorry as I—and Edward, and the whole community in the square, I know—would be to see you return to Richmond, the longer the two of you are parted, the more one can wonder what's going on with you two."

"That long?" Ginny asked, almost defensively. "Why I don't think—"

"Two years. Do you remember what you told me when I found out that Edward wasn't planning to come back here from what was supposed to be a temporary sabbatical—that he was, in fact, in a hospital up north and said he didn't want me to see him in the condition he was in?"

"Yes, but—"

"Yes, but what? You told me that, if I truly cared about him, I should pack, walk out this door, get in my car, and go to him. Didn't you?"

"Yes."

"And do you still think that was good advice?"

"Yes, of course. But this isn't the same."

"If it's not the same, Ginny, maybe you don't care enough for Lenny and should just end it with him. You're wasting away in limbo. If not Lenny, it should be someone else. Paul Prentice over at the Armstrong Inn is sweet on you. I know he is. You know he is too. And he's quite a catch. You know what I think? I think—"

They were interrupted at the moment by the tinkle of the bell over the doorway and the appearance of a middle-aged couple exhibiting every evidence of being tourists. This was confirmed when they asked the most-asked question in any Savannah book store—whether Tom carried copies of *Midnight in the Garden of Good and Evil*. That book, which launched the Kevin Spacey movie on the famous murder case at the Mercer-Williams House just one square over from Chatham Square, had just about put Savannah back on both the tourist and literary maps after several sleepy decades of rest.

Of course Tom had a copy to sell them—in their choice of hardback, paperback, CD, or audio—he'd once even had it in Braille. But when he'd completed that sale, Ginny had moved over to the door, prepared to leave just behind the couple.

"Ginny," Tom called out, and Ginny stopped at the door and turned.

"Tom," she answered, her voice laced with warning, although she couldn't be upset with her well-meaning friend who had only voiced what her mind had been screaming at her for months.

"Just give it some thought, Ginny. We all mean the best for you."

"Yes . . . thanks, Tom. I will think about it. And you take care of yourself too. You look frazzled. Don't let worry about Edward wear you down."

"It's sweet torture, Ginny. I can't help it."

"I know. It's wonderful that he's outlived his prognosis so long. But you need to take care of yourself as well."

As Ginny walked east along West Gordon Street between the bookstore and her own apartment building, deciding that she would wait until after lunch to find Edward James in his SCAD office, she couldn't help but think about what Tom had said concerning her in-limbo relationship with Lenny. She had been trying to avoid thinking about it for some time, which was much easier to do when no one was dangling it in front of her. It wasn't her fault they were in this limbo—well, not really, she rationalized to herself. Lenny had asked her to marry him right after they'd reunited here a decade before— and had gone on asking her for a couple of years. But then he had stopped. And now, if he asked, she probably would say yes—if for no other reason than they had been together so long it seemed the sensible thing to do. But he hadn't mentioned it for some time now.

So, she didn't really know where she and Lenny intersected anymore—at all. But it was less of a hassle just to let it spin out than to try to figure any of it out. She had thought she would miss him terribly for the semester he said he'd be gone. But she was ashamed to admit that, following a short period of being surprised when he wasn't there to respond with an "Umm" when she made a comment, she didn't feel a void in her life when there no longer was a response even that innocuous. She hadn't hardly noticed when his semester-long absence had quadrupled.

She certainly hadn't resolved anything more than before about life without Lenny when she reached the steps leading up to the first floor of her apartment house. The building, which dated back to before the Civil War, had once been a single dwelling, no doubt one of many townhouses of the wealthy rice planters of the surrounding plantations where their families resided when social gatherings brought them all into Savannah. They would not be there much of the year. In the hot, muggy, months, when the rice fields were plagued with malaria-bearing mosquitoes, the planters would have escaped to even higher ground—most to the area of the Great Smokies—than Savannah.

Some time since what those in Savannah called the war of northern aggression, the house had been cut up into apartments. After the war and during Reconstruction, the

37

planters couldn't hold on to their plantations, let alone their townhouses on the Savannah squares. Some houses had survived intact. The Madison family lived in one such on this row. But most of them had been subdivided. The Armstrong Inn at the eastern end of the square on this row had simply put several row houses in a string together, cutting interior doors in the thick brick walls that had separated them—or filling in additions where a sliver of space had originally separated them.

Ginny's building, three stories above an English basement, had been refurbished into three two-bedroom apartments, one per floor, on the upper stories, with a side staircase giving access to all levels. The basement apartment, having only one bedroom, was smaller, because the boiler and storage room were on this level and a staircase descended from the first floor to a hallway on one side the building, giving general access to these rooms and to the door leading out to the back garden. The basement apartment was entered straight from the street via a door under the front porch.

Ginny had inherited her second-floor unit from her aunt, Marie, who had been considered the "angel" of the little community living on the square, a role that Ginny had more or less inherited, if anyone could follow in her aunt's footsteps in this regard. The other three units belonged to Arnie Richards, who lived in the first-floor unit and who took on the role of super himself to save the cost of having anyone else to do it. Of course, this meant maintenance was even more haphazard now than in years past, because Arnie was no longer mobile.

Ginny hadn't learned of his ownership of units other than his own, though, until she had chipped through his initial curmudgeon protective shell and he had begun to confide in her. Samantha Johnson's family now lived in the third-floor unit, having moved from another apartment in the square some years before, and Tony lived in the basement.

Arnie was as old as mud, and he rarely was able to muster up the strength and energy to leave his apartment at all now. Old age, more than any specific malady was catching up with him. Now Samantha came in during her own school lunchtime and fed him a hot lunch, and Ginny checked in on him in the evening and made sure he got a nutritious dinner. Samantha had been doing this for years. Initially, it was a ploy by Ginny and her friends on the square, including an otherwise quite independent Arnie, to ensure that Samantha got a good lunch for free, as she always ate with Arnie. But the tables had slowly turned on who needed looking after for lunch more.

It was lunchtime now, so Ginny wasn't at all surprised to encounter Samantha shutting Arnie's door behind her when Ginny entered the first-floor foyer.

"Hi, Samantha. Did you have a good lunch. How is . . . Samantha, what's wrong? You are in tears."

"Sorry, Ginny. I . . . sorry."

Before Ginny could say more, Samantha had turned and clumped up the stairs, almost stumbling when she clearly wanted to disappear faster than her lame leg would permit.

Ginny looked at Samantha's disappearing back in surprise and concern. She knew she could just go to her own apartment and leave whatever had happened be—but she also knew that she couldn't. These two—all of her friends on the square—meant too much to her to let anything fester. She moved to Arnie's door and knocked on it.

"Arnie, it's me, Ginny. Can I come in for a moment?"

* * * *

"I gave her notice. I thought she'd be relieved, though. How was I to know it would make her bawl?"

"Notice? Oh, Arnie. What went wrong?"

"Nothin' went wrong. It's time. I won't be needing her anymore. Won't be needing you either, so I might as well make it a clean sweep and give you a month's notice too. And it's for her own good. It's what the rest of you should be doing too, if truth be known."

"I don't understand." And she didn't. Ginny was completely confused and she was starting to shake.

"Sit yourself before you fall down. And here, look at these." Arnie was shoving glossy brochures toward Ginny even as she was stumbling back and almost falling into the tapestry-covered platform rocker that Arnie had said was the favorite seat of his long-departed wife, Anne.

"I don't understand," Ginny nonsensically repeated, still in shock, when she was seated and was looking at two brochures, duplicates and both with the photograph of a large mansion with gardens on each side between its walls and a

40

black, iron picket bordering fence. She was so confused she wasn't able to focus on what Arnie had handed her.

"It's nearby. Right over on Whitaker, facing Forsyth Park. I won't even be going much of anywhere."

"Going?"

"Yes, it's time. Way past time if it wasn't for you and Samantha and the others. Forsyth House. Full services. I won't have to move anywhere again between there and the grave. My name's come up. I've been on the list for more than a year, but I didn't see the need to tell any of you before my name came up. They call it a retirement home. But it's really a last-stop nursing home. And that's what I need now."

"Oh, Arnie."

Ginny looked up at the old curmudgeon who had become one of her nearest and dearest friends. She could hardly see him through the tears forming in her eyes.

"I don't know. We can manage—"

"I know you can. But it's long past time that you did. And Samantha. She graduates high school this year. She needs to be free to have a life of her own. You know as well as I do what she always said she wanted to do—what she stopped saying when she started getting bogged down, hemmed in by our needs. We helped her with that leg—and with a college fund, although she don't know about that—and I'm afraid she feels she owes us, that she has to stay with us. And what we meant to do was free her, not trap her."

The tears were rolling down Ginny's face now. It was harsh, but it was the truth. She had known that—and felt the

41

same way for some time now. But she, like others, had been avoiding it—or, more accurately, had approached in only to run quickly away from it. How surprising that Arnie would be the first to face it.

"What did you tell Samantha?"

"Just the part about moving to Forsyth House—and that I wouldn't be needing her stopping in here after the next couple of weeks. I didn't beat her, and I gave her a good reason on why I wouldn't be needing her. But there was really only one way to do it. To let her know that it was done. And it is; it's done."

"Oh, Arnie. Yes, I completely understand—and agree—about moving away from the arrangement with Samantha. But I can . . . you know I can—"

"Yes, I know you can—and that you would. But you don't need to be pinned down like this any more than Samantha does. You've been living betwixt and between yourself too long. And you know what I mean about that, missy. You can jolly well just walk the extra three blocks to visit me from now on. The exercise will do you good. And don't you be visiting me to badger me about your plumbing problems either. What I just might do is leave my part of this dump to you and you can go through life cursing me for that."

Ginny sat there, snuffling quietly in a ridiculous attempt to hide that she was snuffling. But she didn't say anything as she slowly composed herself.

"And you'll notice that there are two brochures. They aren't different; they're identical. And that extra one there

42

concerns something I think needs to be done—and that you're the one to do it. And you'll need to stop that snifflin' and start discussing with me how to get it done. Because that's going to be a whole lot more difficult on you than it was on me when I fired Samantha."

Ginny was trudging as she mounted the stairs to her apartment. All of this drama was really weighing her down. She shouldn't take this so personally—to take so much responsibility on her own shoulders for the well-being of the others living on the square—but she did feel the responsibility. She felt that it had been laid on her shoulders, no matter how lovingly.

When she went into her apartment she walked straight to the nightstand in her bedroom and opened the drawer and extracted the letter that had been handled so many times that the edges were splitting. The lawyer had delivered it to her, here in the apartment, three months after she had moved in, following having inherited it from her aunt, Marie. "My dear Ginny," it read—in words that Ginny could almost recite by memory.

I asked that you not receive this letter until you had lived on Chatham Square long enough to come to love it and the people living there as I have done. I hope that its magic has worked on you as it did on me—and I believe that you are enough a part of me that it has.

I know that when we discussed in the letters we exchanged those last years the "what would happen" when either of us passed on, I said that I would be willing this apartment to the arts college because my association with it has been such an enjoyment to me and because I know that it would be a good steward of properties on the square that I love. So, you undoubtedly were surprised when I left it to you.

I did so, after much contemplation, for several reasons. I believe that I am gifting SCAD by tempting you to move here, as I believe you and the college are a brilliant match. But, primarily, I did so out of concern for my friends living here on Chatham Square. Just the other day, Rose—no doubt sensing that I was keeping my serious illness from her and others on the square—out of the blue sternly told me, in that charming but disarming way she has, that I could not leave the square until I had provided a substitute who would, as she put it, be the "glue" for those I left behind. At that moment, she took me much aback—especially as we hadn't been discussing my leaving the square in any sense of the word.

But she made me think. I did feel responsibility for my fellow residents on Chatham Square, and I had to admit to myself that this burden had been making me very sad—which is not at all the mood in which I wanted to depart this life. And when I thought on what Rose said, my thoughts went to you. I feel that you are so much like me. And I knew that you were not happy in Richmond, even though you would not openly write to me of this.

And thus, I hope you will forgive me, but I am leaving this apartment to you because I hope that you will settle and live here and enjoy the square and its marvelously eclectic collection of residents as I have. Because I think, as Rose said, that you will be the "glue" that helps all of my precious friends now living here, and those to come, hold it all together and because I think you need to be here yourself. I think you are in the need of a little glue too.

If this does not work out for you, please believe that I did it because it has been such a pleasure having you as my niece, even though we only knew of each other through our letters, and that, in you, I leave this life content that I never will have left—because there is so much of me in you.

And, in case you haven't discovered it yet, Arnie Richards is a sweetie under that gruff armor.

Your loving aunt,
Marie

* * * *

"I think he's right, you know. And that he's very brave to be stepping up to this himself. I must say that, from what little I know of Mr. Richards, I'm a bit surprised he's taken the bull by the horns like this. But . . . but, I'm sorry. I shouldn't have said anything. I hope I haven't offended you."

"Offended me? No, Paul, why would you have offended me? I'm the one who should apologize. I shouldn't have just spilled it all out like that. But you were trying so hard to make this a memorable evening—which, of course, it is—and when you asked me why I was being so far away . . ."

Ginny had run out of steam. She really did think she had been the one who had gone out of bounds. But Paul Prentice had made her feel so comfortable and he was such a good listener. Perhaps she could blame it on the fine wine. They'd been served a different one with each gourmet course, and although she'd only sipped, she wasn't used to this much alcohol.

They were sitting in a quiet corner of the dining room at the Armstrong Inn. Paul Prentice, the recently arrived new manager of the boutique hotel and restaurant, had invited her to this dinner tonight two weeks previously, and when he'd done so, she had been delighted to accept.

It wasn't his fault that she'd had this upsetting encounter with Arnie Richards earlier this afternoon and hadn't wanted to do anything after that as much as to retreat to her own apartment, stick her head under a pillow, and pretend that the life she had been drifting along in with her small group of friends on the square had not inevitably started to unravel.

46

"Well, I know that Samantha Johnson—and Mr. Richards, and others for that matter—have been a mission for you and your friends on the square for years. I have no right to intrude."

"Oh, no, Paul, please don't think that way. You're not intruding. You are part of the life of Chatham Square now yourself. We aren't some small, closed clique. Everyone I know here on the square has immediately taken to you. Please, don't be reticent. We will all enjoy your company—and your counsel. That I've shared this issue with you this evening should tell you how easily and well you fit in here."

Paul reached over and took Ginny's hand. She didn't pull it away. Ignoring the last part of what she'd said, Paul took advantage of what she'd said before that.

"I do hope you enjoy my company, Ginny, and that you will give me frequent opportunities for both of us to enjoy each other's company."

As she mounted the stairs to her apartment that evening, Paul having escorted her the half block from the inn to her front door, she felt like she was floating. She hadn't felt as tingly and—how did the Germans put it?—*Gemütlich*—satisfied and comfortable all at once—for some time. That Paul was a real charmer. And she didn't think that this feeling that had come over her was completely the result of the fine wine she'd been drinking. She tried to remember when she'd ever felt that way with Lenny—and she was coming up with a blank on that.

She could hear the telephone ringing in her apartment as she mounted the stairs. She half hoped whoever was calling would give up before she got to the call. She didn't want anything to break into this feeling Paul had given her. But the ringing hadn't stopped when she got to the telephone.

"Ginny? Hello? I almost gave up. I've been calling for hours. But I wouldn't have given up."

"Hello, Lenny," Ginny answered. She tried—probably unsuccessfully—not to have a dull edge to her voice. Her mood had evaporated the instant she'd heard his voice.

There was a bit of silence before Lenny resumed speaking, almost as if she'd popped the exuberance of his mood roaring down the telephone line.

"I can't go along like this any more, Ginny. I know without a doubt now that I want us to be together. Please marry me, Ginny. Come back to Richmond and let's get married. I checked. There's a position for you here in the VCU art department."

Chapter Three

She'd agreed to meet him. He'd called Samantha and told her he had some exciting news and he'd like to meet her at the bench in the square and tell her about it—and she'd said she'd be there as soon as she finished up with Arnie's lunch. She said she had one more afternoon class to attend to at the high school but she had a little time before she had to be back.

She'd sounded a bit despondent, but she'd agreed to see Jeff. That was half the battle.

Jeff was so keyed up that he got to the bench early and just sat there and fidgeted. He heard someone approach, but it was from the west side of the square, not from Arnie's place, so he didn't turn around until the woman spoke. The voice was a rich mildly southern drawl, her words drawn out like honey and spoken with perfect diction.

"Jeffery Turnball? You are Jeffery Turnball, aren't you?"

"Yes ma'am, that's me," Jeff answered. She was a nice enough looking woman. Perhaps in her mid forties. Trim and dressed expensively. The reddish brown of her hair might be a bit too colorful to be real, but on her it looked good.

"Do you mind if a sit?"

"Umm, I'm expecting someone any minute."

"I won't be more than a minute."

"Uh, sorry. Of course you can sit. Rose is the only one with control over sharing the benches here."

He had meant it as a joke, but it had gone right over her head. She looked perplexed.

"Oh, sorry, I thought you might live on the square. Then you'd know that this is the favorite bench of Rose Drayton, who lives in that big house over there. We have a joke about this being Rose's bench."

"I see. I understand. And, yes, I have heard about Rose Drayton. I guess I have a lot of catching up to do."

She sat down and smiled at Jeff, who was giving her a quizzical look.

"You were right. I do live on the square now. I've rented Clay Winthrop's house over there. My name is Helena Jordan, by the way. I know yours, so I guess it's only polite that you know mine too. I write books and am renting here for a year while I work on a novel about Savannah."

"Golly," Jeff said. He knew it wasn't a brilliant response, but at least he'd had enough control not to say "no shit?" which was his first inclination. He knew that Winthrop was a famous poet, but he'd never met a novelist before.

"I guess you could say I'm an interloper on the square," Helena said with a sigh. "Are those people over at the café from the square?"

"Yes, they are. The woman's Ginny Standler. She's a doll maker and teaches over there at SCAD in the Barnard building. And the older, tall, thin man is Mr. James. He's her boss at the school. And the man sitting beside him is his friend, Tom Thornton. He runs the Pitt Bookstore over across the square there. The smaller man joining them—that's Tony. He's a real character. I'll leave it for you to find out more about him for yourself. But you're not an interloper. That's where the people from the square meet a lot. And they're all friendly. All you'd have to do is walk over there and introduce yourself and they'd welcome you to join them and sit down. That's how most of us here get to know each other anyway. Other than ones like me, of course. I didn't come to the square. I've been here all my life."

"All your life?" Helena had turned her eyes on him, and he felt as if she was scrutinizing him harder than before. He saw now that she was a beautiful woman. And her beauty—and her apparent interest in him—had him embarrassed and a bit tongue tied.

"Well, most of it. My dad and I moved here when I was really young."

"Your dad and you? Not your mother too?"

"No . . . she was . . . gone almost before I could remember. But, hey, you knew my name when you came over here . . ."

"Yes. I've been asking around and your name came up. No one's been in Clay's house for some time, and there are a few little things that need to be fixed and repaired. I heard that you were handy and might be interested in some piecework."

"Yes ma'am, I could do that."

"Good. Maybe someday this week you could come by and I could show you what needs to be fixed."

"OK, that would be fine." He had politely answered her, but there was a catch in his voice that made her look at him and then trail back to what had caught his attention. Samantha was coming down the steps of the house where she'd been feeding Arnie Richards his lunch. She wasn't looking out into the square yet, though.

Helena rose, obviously having discerned where Jeff's attention had drifted. She looked away too and saw an older woman walking up to the table at the café where her new neighbors were seated. She had meant to return home after enlisting Jeff's help. That had been something she'd been working on doing for days now, if not weeks. But she was sure that the woman standing at the table was Rose Drayton. She'd seen pictures. She'd made it a high priority to find photos of Rose after Clayton had unexpectedly moved in with the woman. There was a time when Helena had thought she might be moving to Chatham Square under other circumstances. Even into Clayton Winthrop's house. The existence of Rose had come as quite a shock to her.

Helena was well on her way toward the café before Samantha saw Jeff sitting at the bench and moved into the square toward him. The older woman didn't linger at the café. She continued, slowly, on to where she crossed West Gordon at the Armstrong Inn and then turned west. But, having started in the direction of the café, Helena continued. It was time for her to start meeting the neighbors—to start the chore of "fitting in."

"Thanks for meeting me, Samantha," Jeff said as soon as Samantha was within conversational range. "I wanted to talk to someone about it."

"About what?" She seemed a bit distracted and definitely "down" for her. Jeff would have asked her why, but she was being so defensive about people asking her how she was doing and what her plans were of late that he didn't ask that. It was, for certain, what he wanted to know—why he'd really asked her to meet him—but he'd decided to approach it from another angle.

"I got a letter from Georgia State today. Offering me a partial basketball scholarship—for the first year, renewable if I make the team. And they've got a hospitality administration undergraduate degree."

"That's great news."

"My dad and I aren't sure I can swing it yet. He's running the figures."

"I'm sure you'll manage to work it out."

"Georgia State is all the way over in Atlanta."

"Yes, I'd heard that was where it is."

She was being so agreeable. This wasn't exactly how he'd hoped this would go.

"Of course, seeing as how what I want to do is hotel administration, it might be just as good—certainly a lot cheaper—to stay right here. Mr. Prentice at the inn says I can work there and he'd work me up the line. Working at the Armstrong Inn has been my dream anyway. Of course, he says it would be easier to become the manager in time if I had a degree in it. But he also mentioned something about maybe sending me there later if I worked out well at the inn."

"But you'd be giving up basketball. You've always said you wanted to play that in college too."

"There's that, of course," Jeff said after leaving a space of silence that, unfortunately, Samantha didn't fill with more discussion on the options—especially the option of him staying right here in Savannah. After a bit, though, he did speak.

"I suppose you plan on going to SCAD right here and following Ginny in the doll making art." He hadn't wanted to push her on that at all. But she wasn't being a bit of help.

"Yes, maybe. Ginny, of course, can help me get in here. And she's also said she could get me in at VCU in Richmond if I wanted to go north. I've been thinking about the University of Maryland too. But, anyway, I think it's great you've been accepted to Georgia State and you'll have a chance to play basketball there. You've worked hard. You deserve that chance."

Jeff gave up and started trying to dream up another topic—anything that would hold Samantha here on the bench with him for as long as possible. He was miserable, though.

Holding Samantha close seemed not to be something that was going to be possible for very much longer.

* * * *

Rose hadn't sat down at the table at the café, although her neighbors on the square had enthusiastically invited her to and Ginny had even said there was something she wanted to talk to her about—just the two of them.

"It's wonderful to see you out and about," Ginny said, as Tom, Edward, and Tony all murmured their agreement.

"I can't sit," she said. "The doctor is with Clayton and he ordered me to take a walk around the block. He doesn't fool me, though. He thinks I'm putting on too much weight."

"I don't think . . . ," Ginny started to say, but then she switched gears. "But, here, let me walk with you. We can have a little chat while we're walking."

"You've just gotten that drink, Ginny. And . . . uh, I have an errand to run too."

Ginny choked off what she had been about to say. Rose almost never got out. There obviously was something she wanted to do alone. And Ginny was the last one who would want to prevent her from doing that.

"But it's so nice to see you out in the square, Edward," Rose said. "It's been some time . . . and Tom. You need to get out more, dear."

"As do you," Tom replied.

And then Rose had moved on, and the attention of those at the table went to the well-dressed, perfectly coiffured auburn-haired woman approaching them from the park.

"Ah, the new, mysterious novelist of Chatham Square, I presume, come at last for us to genuflect and kiss her hand," Tony murmured in his best Bette Davis voice.

"Behave, Tony," Ginny muttered. "Let's not overwhelm her all at once."

Rose gave no heed to what was going on at the café behind her. She hadn't had to come out, although the doctor had tutted and told her she needed to be taking care of herself better. But she was on a mission—and it hadn't been easy to schedule a time when she could talk with Rodney Johnson alone. She had researched when that would be and had scheduled the doctor's visit accordingly.

Rodney played trumpet nights at one of her jazz venues downtown. His wife, Jasmine, would be contending with the luncheon crowd at the Armstrong Inn. And, as Rose planned and could see was happening, their daughter, Samantha, had just finished feeding Arnie Richards his lunch and had come out to the bench to talk with that nice young man, Jeff Turnball.

Rose was pleased to see that Samantha and Jeff were spending time together. She thought they made a lovely couple—and she hoped they didn't mess around like she had done in getting around to seeing that they went well with each other. Rose hoped that Jeff was getting the preparation he needed to have enjoyable work and enough to support the two of them. She reminded herself to look into that and consider what she might do to help.

And this brought to mind what she was out on the square to do today. She had clumped past the stairs up to the Armstrong Inn and was bearing down on the apartment house where the Johnsons lived on the top floor. Her cane was making a determined tap, tap sound on the brick walk as mostly by stubborn will, she moved along, trying to cover how painful and exhausting this was for her to accomplish.

The three-flight climb to the landing outside the Johnson's door just about did her in, and she had to stand out there, leaning on her cane and the banister of the stairs, for a good ten minutes before she could compose herself and catch her breath.

Rodney Johnson was the perfect host, not even showing surprise and alarm to find Rose knocking at his door. The Johnsons and the Draytons went way back—and somewhere back in that history there was a relationship that the Drayton clan had no reason to be proud of. But that had evaporated long before Rose and Rodney had been born. Rose's father had employed Rodney's father and given him both the respect and the salary that still wasn't expected by a black man in the mid-twentieth-century South. And Rose, in turn, having seen the musical talent Rodney had shown, had made sure that he had a seat on the bandstand in one or more of her clubs. She'd even stuck with him when he'd had a patch of feeling so sorry for himself that he'd gone to drink.

But when his daughter needed him, he'd pulled up his bootstraps and gone to New Orleans, where the jazz clubs were open night and day. And he'd done that so he could work night and day. Because he'd promised his daughter he'd fix her leg.

Many in the square had thought that Samantha's medical condition was just too much responsibility for him to bear and that he'd abandoned his hotel maid wife and daughter. But Rose had always known better. She had known where he was and what he was doing—and when he was needed the most, she saw that he could come home. What he'd brought home wasn't nearly enough to pay for the operations Samantha had needed. But it was enough for everyone to know that he'd worked himself almost to death and denied his own needs. And, added to what the people of the square had pulled together—and what the surgeon and medical staff also contributed in gratis services—it had been enough. Samantha's leg would never be perfect—but it would never again hold her back.

That being the case—Rodney Johnson being the man that he was—Rose had no doubt how her visit to him today would end up. But she'd promised Ginny she'd talk with him.

"Yes, thank you for asking, Ms. Rose," Rodney said, as he poured her the cup of tea that was so weak that Rose could hardly distinguish it from water, and held out the plate of cookies, some of which were broken, none of which looked homemade to her. None of that mattered. Rodney was being the perfect host. And Rose was determined to be the perfect guest.

"We are talking with our Samantha about what she wants to do. We don't want to press, and she still seems to be undecided. But when she decides, we'll likely tell her that's a good idea. Our Samantha doesn't have anything but good ideas."

"She once said she wanted to become a doctor. And she'd be wonderful at that."

"Yes, ma'am. My Jasmine and me think she'd be real fine at that too. And if that's what she wants to do, why that's what we'll work on."

"Medical school on top of a good undergraduate college is very expensive, I've heard."

"Yes, ma'am, it surely is. But we've put aside enough for her to get started on that, if that's what she wants. And if that's what she wants, we'll find a way. But thank you kindly for asking."

"Yes, I'm sure you will, Rodney," Rose answered.

That's as far as she took that topic. Rodney Johnson's pride and determination were shining through so hard that she couldn't help but seeing them—and both Rodney and she knew what she was suggesting. And they knew what Rodney Johnson's answer was to that.

"You and the others in the square have been wonderful to Samantha—and to Jasmine and me too," Rodney said. "We can never be grateful enough for what you've done for our girl—how you've helped us all fit in here. You all helped us get to where we could take care of ourselves again."

"And that puts the slammer on that," Rose thought. She turned then to pleasantries, saying that she had been meaning to visit for some time and was so sorry that she'd picked a time when Jasmine and Samantha weren't there too—and that maybe the three of them could come visit her and Clayton across the square someday soon.

Yes, indeed, they would have to do that, Rodney said, going along with the charade, although he'd known exactly what Rose's visit was all about—although there was no reason for him to have known that a college fund already existed. He also knew that it was highly unlikely that his family would be visiting Rose's house on the square. The last two generations of the Draytons had been wonderful to his family. But there were some divides that folks just didn't cross. And it wasn't always because they wouldn't be welcome to cross them. Sometimes it was a matter of their own pride.

Rose wasn't displeased as she slowly let herself down the stairs—having told Rodney Johnson the lie that it would be no trouble for her to do so. She would tell Ginny that Samantha's parents knew that help was available. If Ginny wanted to take that as having told them about the college fund, that was to the good. But Rose could see—and understand— the pride in Rodney Johnson. That's why she'd helped him go to New Orleans all those years ago and find work and let people in the square have the false impression that he'd run away. The pride she saw in his eyes when he came home with a wad of money to "fix his little girl" was worth the effort she'd put in to help him earn that money—and didn't deny the hard work required for him to do so. After he'd returned, her efforts had gone—successfully, she thought—into him not knowing just how short the distance his hard-earned money went to the goal of "fixing" Samantha's leg.

This, she knew, was another case of whatever the Johnsons had scraped together being enough to give Samantha a start until she reached eighteen and learned that there was far more available to help her.

The effort now needed to be in trying to make sure that what Samantha chose to pursue was what she really wanted and not what those around her needed from her. This would be one of the hardest projects Rose had ever taken on, because she realized that freeing Samantha to follow her dream likely ended Rose's own dreams.

* * * *

"You said 'when you move back to Richmond.' You are decided on that, then?"

Paul Prentice was trying not to sound disappointed. He had arrived at William's Café just as the kaffee-klatsch was breaking up. These meetings of the people of the square at the café were hit-and-miss and unorchestrated events. This one had been more interesting than most—and lasted longer into the afternoon than most as well—because they'd had the novelist Helena Jordan to work on deciphering. She was

61

pleasant enough and wasn't the least bit snobby, but she also was pretty secretive. Ginny and the others shared glances that assured them all that there was more to the story of Helena Jordan arriving in Chatham Square than was showing on the surface. But the woman was talented at both tantalizing them and fending them off at the same time—and without being unpleasant.

Helena had moved on to another table in the café, drawn there by Tony. The two had, surprisingly, hit it off wonderfully, and Tony was so taken with her that he wanted to introduce her to other patrons at the café. The table where they had landed was occupied by two other recently settled residents of the square, both young professionals living in small apartments in buildings originally built as town mansions and now cut up into more economical—and much smaller—cubby-hole apartments. The young woman, if Ginny remembered correctly, was a teacher at Samantha's high school. And the young man at the table was a real estate broker. Ginny had yet to meet them, but before long she knew that they would be fully integrated in what she considered to be "her generation" of Chatham Square residents.

Ginny sighed at the thought that even here, in this remote Savannah square, life went on in cycles. It had done so for nearly three centuries, and the advance in age of most, and coming of age of some of those who had been here to greet her when she'd arrived ten years earlier were both a bittersweet and heartening reminder of the relentless movement of time.

When Paul arrived, Ginny told him that she was about to leave to get back to work on her dolls, being the last one remaining from the group interrogation of Helena Jordan. Paul voiced his regret, saying that the luncheon service at the Armstrong Inn had been both more difficult and more time consuming than he had anticipated. And he begged Ginny to remain for a bit—at least long enough for him to have coffee and some pleasant company before he had to return to the inn and start preparing for the arrival of new guests and the supper hour.

What he gleaned from Ginny when they began to chat, however, was more unsettling than pleasant.

"Yes. I'm not sure whether I'll go in time for the coming semester or before the next one. But there's a position available for me at VCU again, and I've been away from my boyfriend too long already. And there will be wedding plans to make, of course."

She laid that out there on the table between them, and hers was a mixture of pleasure and regret to see that it caused a shadow of gloom to go across Paul's face. She liked Paul—a lot. And she wasn't as decided as she was letting on. She was actually practicing this for Samantha. It was hard to paint this scenario for Paul when it seemed—and his demeanor confirmed—that something had been developing between them.

But it would be much harder to play this scene with Samantha. Arnie had humbled her and spurred her to action. And she now saw that her needling of Rose on this point had been hypocritical. She hadn't been any less prone to dragging her feet in urging Samantha to spread her wings beyond Chatham Square than Rose had been.

Yes, after a long hiatus in offers, Lenny had finally proposed again—no, begged her to marry him and come to him in Richmond. Yes, she had been weighing these proposals for years—and had started to welcome them when they stopped. But that was before Paul Prentice had come to the Armstrong Inn. Now she was confused and wasn't at all sure she wanted to go to Richmond or to marry Lenny. But it was a scenario that would work with Samantha to close out the possibility of the two of them combining to start up an art doll company right here.

This had been a dream of hers and in recent years she had convinced herself that it was dream of Samantha's too. But now Ginny could see that it was a dream of convenience for Samantha because it would mean that she could continue being the main support for all of those people of the square that she felt beholden to for seeing that she got those operations on her leg. Ginny didn't want Samantha to remain here for that reason. She—and she knew the others, as well—hadn't done that for Samantha to enslave herself to them. They had done it because Samantha was a wonderful girl who had promise—and because she needed the help.

And Ginny couldn't forget that for many years Samantha had said she wanted to become a doctor. There was no denying, either, that Samantha had a calling to be a healer.

As hard as it would be, the easy part would be making Samantha believe that Ginny was moving away from her no matter what Samantha decided to do with her life. The hard part would be in lying to Samantha and telling her that she didn't have a career in textile art. That would break Ginny's heart to do, because the young woman was extraordinarily gifted in the art that Ginny loved—achingly so, when Ginny compared her own talent to Samantha's.

"But there's no change in the immediate future then," Paul was saying.

"No, I won't be leaving for several months yet."

"Good," Paul said. And when Ginny looked into her eyes, she saw the aching hopefulness there.

Chapter Four

Jeff Turnball was making a half-hearted effort at drying the lunch dishes he had just washed, but his attention wasn't on them. His eyes kept going to his dad, who was sitting in his shirt sleeves at their small dining table, with reams of paper and a calculator spread out in front of him. Jim Turnball was due back at the grocery store for the second of the two shifts he was working that day, but he had told Jeff he couldn't concentrate at work until he'd gone over the figures on how they were going to work out Jeff's education costs if he went off to Georgia State.

Jim was hunched over the papers and calculator and his shoulders had fallen, both of which signaled that the calculations just weren't going Jeff's way.

"Why don't you leave that for later, Dad?" Jeff called out softly. The basement apartment was small enough that there was no needed to raise one's voice to reach from one end of the unit to the other. "You need to get back to work, and that can wait."

"I don't know. I just don't know." Jim pulled his eyeglasses away from his face and rubbed he eyes. Jeff could see the deep tension lines caused by the frustration.

"You know, I've been thinking," Jeff said, putting the tea towel down and coming over and taking up the pile of papers and sifting them together into one neat pile, thereby effectively ending his father's agony over them not telling him what he wanted to see in them. "Maybe it would be good for me to get some experience under my belt at the inn before going off for that hospitality management degree. I could probably do a lot better in school—could find it all so much easier—if I had more practical experience first."

"I don't know. You think?" It wasn't an optimistic tone Jim was using. He knew as well as Jeff did that this particular basketball scholarship was a one-time deal. If that passed Jeff by, it would be that much harder to come up with the money needed to cover the college program.

"Let's leave it for now, Dad. We've got time to work something out."

"Not much time. Uh, by the way, we've got a special on for honey-baked hams at the store. I have half a notion to get one. But they're all too big for our needs. That's reminded me that we discussed something about inviting that girl you're sweet on, Samantha Johnson, over for dinner. How's it coming with her?"

"Not all that great, Dad. I'm just about out of ideas on that."

"Well, why don't you invite her anyway? She's a nice girl—and this neighborhood can't get along without her. I think it would be nice to let her know how much she's appreciated around here. How about tomorrow night? You think that's too soon?"

"Can't tomorrow. I'm rehanging the doors on Ms. Jordan's kitchen cabinets. And she's asked me to stay for dinner there after I'm done. I thought you were working through dinner tomorrow night and wouldn't be home anyway."

"I can make adjustments at the store. You've been over at Helena Jordan's pretty often in the last two weeks. Any particular attraction over there?"

"Now don't you start ragging me on that too, Dad."

"Ragging you? How?" Jim's face took on a look of complete innocence, and maybe his remark had actually been that—innocent.

"Some of the other guys at the grocery store have been mouthing stuff about her robbing the cradle and all that—that maybe she has an interest in me that goes beyond fixing things. But it's not that. I find her interesting, yes—a lot more interesting than that Seldon woman living with her—but I just fix things and we talk a bit. I'm not interested in her that way. And although she sits and watches me work sometimes, I don't think she has thoughts like the guys say either. I asked her about that, and she said she studies people for the characters in her novels. So, maybe someday I'll see myself in one of her novels."

"It wouldn't surprise me if you did. But you like her, you say."

"Yeah I guess I do. Is it OK for a younger guy to just like to talk with an older woman?"

"It's OK. I'm sort of glad you like her," Jim answered.

Jeff found that remark a little cryptic, and he was about to ask his father about it, but Jim had already risen from the table and was working his way toward the door.

"Don't worry about the college, son. If you want to start there in the fall, we'll work something out. You can't get something completed by not having the courage to start it. The Kroger people have been talking to me about managing one of their new stores out toward Tybee Island. It would be quite a bit more money, and the rents out that way are cheaper than here too."

"But you love the store you're working at, Dad. You're always saying it has that small neighborhood feel to it and that you love working where you know all of the customers. And we'd have to move away from the square. And the people here on the square like having you at the store too. Who's to say the home delivery program will continue if you leave, too? People like Ms. Rose and Mr. Richards have come to rely on that."

"If you go to Georgia State, you'll have to move away from the square anyway, and the home delivery depends mostly on you, although I guess I could get another guy to do it," Jim answered. "And maybe it's time I moved on too. We would be doing better if I had taken more of the opportunities like the one Kroger is offering."

"If you're looking for your books, you'll find them up front on the table by the door. You're increasingly being 'found' on the square, and I've bowed to the inevitable. It's a chase when a tourist comes through the door now on whether they want *Midnight in the Garden of Good and Evil* or one of your books. And I'm forever pointing out which house is yours. If I don't like the look of them, though, I point to the wrong one."

"I'm sorry to have become a bother to you," Helena Jordan said, "But it's flattering to be up there on the front table."

"It's no bother. We're honored to have a novelist of your reputation on the square—and especially so from the book sales perspective. And oh, sorry," he said, turning to Jane Seldon, who had come into the Pitt Bookstore with Helena, "you asked for cookbooks. They're in that section over there. Go down that aisle, and way in the back of the store."

Tom was happy that Helena and her friend had come into the shop. Samantha was in the upstairs apartment taking Edward's blood pressure and other vital signs, and Tom always held his breath during that routine. For several years now, he had dreaded the day she came down the stairs and told him that perhaps they should call for an ambulance.

He had had no idea that someone could live this long with a heart transplant. When he had driven north a decade ago, it was with the understanding that he was on his way to his lover's deathbed. The doctors had certainly told Edward—

and him—that this would be the result in a matter of weeks if a heart wasn't found for Edward—that there was no more they could do with just replacing valves or changing his pacemaker. And that it would be touch and go even then. But then, miracle of miracles, a heart had been found and successfully transplanted and Edward was smashing all predictions by hanging in there.

But Tom was a realist. He knew that it was just a matter of time—for all of them. Thus, whenever Samantha visited to check on Edward, Tom sat down in the bookstore, his own heart palpitating, clothed in worry over how Edward was doing.

Tom's heart had been palpitating a lot recently, and there had been brief moments when his arm felt numb. He didn't want to impose on Samantha to check him out too. Perhaps, he was thinking when Helena and her companion entered the store, he should schedule a checkup with a doctor himself.

"So, are you just visiting your books or are you helping your friend pick out a cookbook?"

Tom had turned back to Helena. He met her only a week or so earlier, when she introduced herself at William's Café, but he had taken an instant liking to her. This impression probably should have been tarnished when the gossip had reached him that she was showing quite a bit of interest in the Turnball boy, who was young enough to be her son. But Tom knew he was among the last of the people on the square who should be concerned about conventions. He would accept Helena Jordan at face value just as his neighbors had accepted

71

him and Edward. It wasn't any of his close friends who were saying anything.

Jeff Turnball could just watch out for himself—if he wanted to.

Tom was slightly more concerned about Rose and Clayton. Clayton Winthrop had talked to Tom on occasion about Helena Jordan and his close friendship with the novelist in the years before he and Rose "found" themselves again. And Clayton had rented his house to Helena.

Tom didn't know if Helena had found Clayton here in Savannah or if it had been the other way around. When Clayton had first started to develop liver problems, he had come to Tom to ask him for help in researching the circle of literary friends he had moved in after returning from the Vietnam war. He'd spent considerable time in New York City, where his own fame as a poet had been established, not least because of the literary connections he kept there. That, apparently, is where he'd met Helena Jordan.

Tom had tracked down contact information about her and others, and in the past couple of years, many of Clayton's old friends in the arts had been stopping by. It was morbid to think so, but it was quite evident that Clayton was hosting a "last round" of visits with his colleagues.

Helena was one of those old friends. But she wasn't just visiting. She had moved in.

While Tom was researching, he came across references in old newspapers and magazines that indicated that Clayton and Helena had once been more than "just

72

friends." Tom was much too fond of Rose—despite having taken a liking to Helena as well—not to worry why Helena was here.

He almost wished there was something developing between the Turnball boy and the novelist.

Once thing that Tom did know was that he didn't much care for Helena's companion, Jane Seldon, who was the whiney and clingy type. She was quite good looking and at least a decade younger than Helena, so there might be something there between those two. And again, Tom thought, that would be miles better than what he was afraid of.

When Tom asked Helena if she was looking for a book too, she said, "Oh, yes, I'm the one who suggested we drop in to the bookstore. Do you happen to have any books on college admissions, you know, something that would give summaries of colleges and courses in study and contact names and numbers?"

"Why, yes, of course. Right over there on that table. This is the time of year when students are coming in looking for that. But now it's freshmen and sophomores coming in rather than juniors and seniors. It seems time is moving ahead ever faster, even here in Savannah. Were you thinking of teaching courses?"

"Umm, that's a thought, isn't it? I'll just take one of these, thanks. It looks like it has the information I'll want."

As he rang the sale up, he summoned the courage to ask her what he'd wanted to ask her ever since he'd heard she was moving into Clayton Winthrop's house on the square. "Do you have a new book coming out soon? If so, perhaps we could arrange a city launching and book signing here."

"Umm?"

Tom didn't think Helena was listening to him. She was at his front window and seemed to be staring intently out at something on the square. So he repeated himself.

"I have something almost out in pen name. It's called *By the Howling*. But it won't be until the winter when my next novel comes out."

"And perhaps we could have a special signing of that then?"

"Umm. Yes, of course, that would be wonderful. And certainly when the novel I'm working on now—one about Savannah—is ready, I would love to launch it right here."

Helena was responding as she should, but her rich, velvety voice with just a hint of southern drawl still had a faraway quality to it. Tom moved to where he could look past her out of the window and try to see what she saw.

What she was looking at was Rose, tapping along the brick walk in the center of the square, but not stopping there, moving north, deeper into the historical district.

"Excuse me. I've just remembered that I have another errand to run. I don't want to interrupt Jane. When she starts looking into cookbooks, she's lost to the world. When she comes up for air, would you tell her I'll see her at home—and remind her for me, please, that there will be three for dinner tonight. Oh, and can I leave this purchase for Jane to take home?"

Tom answered that he would do all that Helena had asked, but he was still watching the receding back of Rose Drayton as she left the square and started walking downtown on Whitaker. Every fiber in his body was screaming, "Don't, Rose. Return to your house." But then any thoughts of Rose were replaced with a dull pain under his sternum and a tingling sensation in his left arm.

* * * *

This was one of Clayton's good days—one of his really good days. He had pulled himself out of his bed in the study and into a wheelchair and had wheeled himself out to the parlor and to one of the tall front windows.

"I wanted to see the azaleas in the square," he told Rose. "They don't last all that long, so you have to take them in while they're here."

"You seem really spry today."

"Yes, I feel quite good. Perhaps before you go out you could make sure there is some blank paper and sharp pencils at the desk over there. I have a few more poems in my head that are crying to get out. I have to let them have their way on a day as good as this."

"Go out? I wasn't thinking of going out. Samantha isn't coming today."

"It's such a beautiful day—and I'm feeling quite well. There aren't many chances like this. Surely you have some

75

personal shopping you'd like to do. If not, why not just take a walk?"

"Well, if you think you can cope."

"Of course I can cope."

Rose got the impression that Clayton couldn't get his poems down on paper if he felt her presence in the house, so, of course, as disappointing as that was, she'd find something to do. She would go to the grocery store and see if Jim Turnball had any exotic fruits in. She never listed them on her grocery requests, because she had no idea what was in season.

Clayton waited until Rose had left and then he wheeled over to the telephone table, opened the drawer, and pulled out the Savannah telephone book. He searched around in the folds of the throw across his legs and came up with his wallet. He'd need his credit cards for a couple of these calls.

He'd only made two of calls, though, before he heard the doorbell chime.

When Rose returned nearly an hour later, she heard the laughter before she'd even opened the door, and thus was prepared for what she'd find. She had been expecting this.

Clayton and Helena Jordan were sitting at the tea table, with cups of tea and a plate of cookies between them.

Clayton couldn't have reached those himself, Rose mused. Helena Jordan had quickly made herself at home here. Rose had visions of Helena Jordan moving around in her kitchen—maybe even wearing one of her aprons—and she didn't like that vision one bit. Rose wondered whether the Jordan woman had been lurking in the bushes for days, waiting

76

for Rose to leave the house, or whether having the woman over was the reason Clayton had pushed her out of the house.

Clayton made the introductions, although that was only superficially needed by both of the women. Both Rose and Helena had checked each other out a long time ago.

When Helena rose from the tea table, it was to the great relief of both women, although Clayton didn't seem to have felt the frost in the air.

"Well, I must be running. It was great to see you again, Clayton—and to meet you, Rose."

"Must you go? You certainly seemed to have cheered Clayton up." The words were gracious, although Rose was fighting to keep her expression benign.

"And probably tired him out in the process. I shouldn't stay long, I know. I'll visit again soon."

"Yes, please do." Rose credited herself for not having coated her statement in ice. She, in fact, knew she should be pleased by whatever made Clayton laugh and forget the world he had come to know in the last two years.

After seeing Helena out at the door, Rose turned, looked across the room, and saw that the telephone book was out. Working her way closer to the table, she could see the page it was opened to.

So, it had come to this? She guessed it was inevitable. Ginny had been hinting about it too. Rose felt so selfish. Life on the square had finally become what she had dreamed it would be. Life just wasn't fair.

"Come, sit with me, Rose. Please. I'm having so few lucid moments that I must cherish and take advantage of each one. There's something I want to discuss with you."

"Yes, of course, Clayton," she answered. "But let me warm the tea pot first."

"Don't be long. I wouldn't want to be snoring when you came back."

Rose almost burst into tears then. She lived to hear Clayton snoring these days. It meant his sleep was saving him from perpetual pain. It meant he was sleeping well, not moaning as he usually did in a half stupor that gave neither one of them rest. Rose longed these days to hear him snore—it was a lullaby that allowed her to sleep as well.

Before she turned to pick up the tea pot and head for the kitchen, she flipped the telephone book shut. She had no wish to know that it was opened to mortuaries while she and Clayton sipped tea and she begged him to read to her from the poetry collection he was putting together—knowing he would refuse to do so until it was all together, but also knowing that he'd be pleased that she had asked.

In truth she could wait to hear the poems read from this last book of his, because she knew when the book was finished, Clayton would be gone.

* * * *

"Here. I think she's ready to have her face painting finished. I did most of it last night, but I saved the eyes for you. You've always been magic with the eyes."

Ginny had stayed up much of the previous night, working on the Scottish doll and fretting over what to say to Samantha when she came downstairs to work with Ginny in the doll room this afternoon. It was Friday, the day Samantha didn't have to return to school for classes after preparing Arnie's lunch on the floor below.

This was a ritual—on Mondays, Wednesdays, and Fridays—that had gone back years—to when Samantha's family was having a hard time making ends meet and paying the bills on Samantha's leg operations. It was touch and go with them, even when they didn't realize what bills the surgeon was sending to Rose instead of them, and there were far more bills than either Samantha or her parents knew about. The residents of the square—mainly Rose, Ginny, Clayton, Tom, and Tony—had banded together a decade earlier and each, in their own way, had contributed to a fund to help with Samantha's medical expenses. Most of the money had been raised through various community projects, so one could really say that all of Savannah had mobilized to help Samantha walk better.

It was then—after Samantha had recovered from the major surgeries required—that Ginny had hired her to help make art dolls. Ginny taught textile art and doll making at SCAD, with her dolls selling for well up to $3,000 apiece. She had more orders than she could keep up with, so hiring

79

someone to help her wasn't an act of charity. And hiring Samantha to help her wasn't an act of charity either; Samantha had proved to be highly talented at doll making. But it did help the Johnsons cover their bills. And it also helped them with their grocery costs, because at the same time a routine started where Samantha made Arnie's lunch every weekday—doing the shopping for him too until Jeff Turnball took over direct deliveries from his dad's store—and three days a week she ate dinner at Ginny's after working three or four hours in the studio Ginny had set up in her spare bedroom.

Today had been like most every other Friday. Ginny had heard Samantha leave Arnie's apartment downstairs and then go up to the third floor to leave off her books and change her clothes. And then her footsteps brought her back down to Ginny's second-floor apartment.

All the time Ginny heard the young woman moving around she'd been composing her "you're fired" speech. She couldn't bring herself to do it as abruptly as Arnie had done it. But Ginny knew she was being selfish by not taking all of the obstacles away from Samantha going away someplace to study medicine. There was no good premed college course near Savannah. Ginny had already checked on that.

No, something needed to be done to turn Samantha away from a possible future of staying here with Ginny in the doll business. And Ginny intended to start doing it today.

As it happened, though, Samantha was the first one to bring the issue up.

"Arnie tells me you are planning to return to Richmond."

80

"Yes, there's a position for me there at VCU, and Lenny has proposed."

"He seems to have taken a long time to do that. Men can be quite confusing, and it's hard to know what to do—what to look for in a man, isn't it?"

Ginny laughed, although she remembered to put her hand on Samantha's as the young woman had picked up a panel of a gown for a Jackie Kennedy doll and take the cloth from Samantha. "Here, this other panel should be sewn in first."

There, of course, was no reason why one panel should not have been sewn in before any other, but Ginny had to start building doubt in Samantha's mind on doll making some place.

"Yes, men can be difficult to figure out—and to be assessed for marriage potential and interest. But you have plenty of time to think about that, Ms. Johnson. Here, use this thread instead. It's less coarse, and I don't think you have the shade just right with that strand."

"Uh, sorry. I don't think I'll be any older than I am to be confused about men, though."

Something in the way Samantha had said that made Ginny stop and look over at her. "This wouldn't be about Jeff Turnball and William Madison, would it?"

"Yes, ma'am, it might be. I just don't know—and coming at a time when I have to think about what I want to do next year . . . I just don't know."

"There's no reason why you need to be worrying about choosing men either this or next year, but there is a reason to think about what you want to do in life from now. My suggestion would be to do that first and let the boys take care of themselves for a while. Have you thought of getting away altogether?"

"Yes, ma'am, I have. And with you going to Richmond, there's maybe VCU."

"Oh, I'd suggest you get away from everyone you know for a year or two. Really spread your wings and do something entirely different. Even get away from these dolls. Here, mind the hairdo on that doll. We wouldn't want to have to work on that again."

Ginny couldn't look at Samantha to catch what her reaction was to the "getting away from everyone" suggestion. Until now, Ginny had been pushing a bit on Samantha to go either to SCAD or VCU to train with Ginny further in the doll making field. But now Ginny was beginning to shut the door on that. Samantha was a smart girl; Ginny knew that the young woman would be hearing the door starting to shut on that possibility.

"William wants me to stay here and go to SCAD where he's going. And Jeff . . . I don't know about him. He's talking about staying here and working at the inn or going to Georgia State. I just don't know."

"Well, I'd suggest not choosing what you do to meet their expectations—especially as you don't sound like you are particularly partial to one over the other. You aren't, are you?"

"Well . . . no, not really. William would be logical choice, for several reasons."

"But since you can't just flatly say it's William, you haven't made up your mind, have you?"

"No. But have you? I know you've been with Lenny a lot. But when I see you and Paul Prentice together . . ."

"Ah, well. I'm a good bit older, you know. I need to be sensible in ways that you needn't bother with at your age." Ginny could feel her cheeks burning. Was her attraction to Paul Prentice that noticeable to others?

"Anyway, I remember you saying you wanted to be a doctor, and I know you'd be a terrific one. You haven't given up on that dream, have you? And, if you haven't, you need to find a good university somewhere that leads to a good medical school." Now if that didn't signal Samantha to turn away from studying doll art, Ginny didn't know what else she could do—other than continue to criticize her work.

"Yes, I've been thinking about that too," Samantha said in a faraway voice.

This was when Ginny picked up the nearly complete Scottish doll. "Here. I think she's ready to have her face painting finished. I did most of it last night, but I saved the eyes for you. You've always been magic with the eyes."

Both women held their breath and put their heads together as, holding the doll's face toward the light of the only window in Ginny's spare room, Samantha charged the tiny brushes with the paints she needed and concentrated on the porcelain figure she held in a steady grip.

When she was done, Ginny could hardly see her work through the tears forming in her eyes. "They're perfect, Samantha. You've made her come alive."

It wasn't anything like she had been determined to tell Samantha. But what Samantha had done with the Scottish doll with just a few deft strokes and subtle layering of the paint was exquisite. Ginny was an artist. She couldn't lie to another artist—an artist who was potentially a much greater artist that she herself would ever be.

* * * *

Samantha felt a panic such as she never had felt before. She didn't quite know how she'd gotten in this situation. She felt guilty that it was something that she'd done—that she'd somehow signaled to William that she was ready for this, wanted this.

They were in the dark alley behind the southern rank of townhouses on Chatham Square, parked up against the double doors of the Madison's garage at the rear of their townhouse. Dim lights shone over the garages and parking pads of other houses down and up the line, but the one above the Madison's garage was out. She wondered, nonsensically, if William had taken the bulb out—if he had planned this.

"William. Please. I didn't mean for this—"

"Come on, don't tease, Sam. We've been going out for months now. We're practically engaged."

"William, no. Please."

She was wedged in the passenger seat of William's Miata convertible and William was leaning in toward her, moving his hands everywhere. Even inside her blouse and under her bra. This had never happened to her before.

She struck out and connected with his nose with the heel of her hand, which caused him to cry out in pain and pull away from her.

"Ow. What did you do that for? Come on. You know you want it."

"No, I most certainly do not want this, William Madison. You're drunk. I told you not to drink that much at the party. This isn't like you."

She jerked off her seat belt and opened her door and had one foot on the ground.

"Hey. Where are you goin'? Come back here. Don't be a tease."

"I'm going home, William. Are you going to be a gentleman and walk me home now? You've had too much to drink. I bet you don't remember this in the morning."

"If you were nice to me, we'd both remember it. I'll treat you real good."

Samantha stood beside the car, adjusting her clothes as best she could, but her hands were trembling. She'd never been so scared—and so mad—all at the same time.

"Are you going to make me walk home alone down this dark alley?"

There was no response. William was withdrawing into himself, pouting.

This was the first time that William had drunk so much beer at a party he'd taken her to. She'd upset him there, she knew. He'd been pawing her, obviously wanted to show his friends the totality of his possession of her, and she had pushed him away. But that alone shouldn't have made him go on a drinking binge, she didn't think. His friends didn't seem to notice that she was being a bit standoffish. So, again she searched her mind and her behavior this evening, wondering what she had done wrong to cause this. It must be her fault. William was such a gentleman. Well, until just now.

As near as she could remember, he hadn't changed when she wouldn't let him pet her in public. He'd gone silent and pouty on her and started drinking heavier when she'd asked him about when he was going to introduce her to his parents. He'd been after her again about registering at SCAD, where he studied architecture, so that they could be together, saying they were almost engaged.

But when she'd mentioned meeting his parents, he got all defensive and then touchy again and, finally, tipsy.

While he was driving home—refusing to give her the keys so she could drive—he was telling her how beautiful she was and then how sexy she looked—and how much he wanted her—so that by the time they were parked in the alley behind his house, he was saying how much he loved her and how he couldn't hold out any longer to be with her. And since they were practically married anyway . . .

Samantha had been overwhelmed. And as she carefully worked her way over the cobblestones of the alley in her high heels toward the back gate of her own apartment house, she tried to compose herself and get control of her breath. She knew her father or mother—most likely both—would be waiting up for her. And if she showed them how upset she was, they'd want to know why.

It was just because he'd been drinking. She never knew him to get like this before. But it certainly started doubts racing through her brain, and she had no idea how she could face him and look at him in the same way as before.

It was all so confusing and so, so terrible. Life was just falling apart around her. She wanted it to be like it always had been on the square. But she knew it never again would be so.

* * * *

Ginny was fixing herself a cup of tea before going to bed. She had no idea what thoughts of getting away from Chatham Square she had instilled in Samantha's brain earlier in the evening. But she had been an utter failure at starting a campaign to wave the young woman away from a life in the arts. Whether or not Samantha became a doctor, she was an extraordinarily talented artist, and Ginny simply could not bring herself to pretend otherwise.

But while she had been attempting to guide Samantha's choices, Samantha had managed to rip open Ginny's own heart. At dinner, the topic of Paul Prentice had come up again, and everything that was forming in Ginny's mind was enlarging the image of Paul and diminishing that of Lenny. She couldn't fool herself; she wasn't nearly as sure of a decision to return to Richmond and marry Lenny as she was letting on.

But she couldn't think of that now. She had a class to teach in the morning, and all of this stress of trying to manipulate Samantha—if she was honest, she had to admit that this was what she was trying to do, and she wasn't the least bit comfortable doing it—had placed a dull, pounding headache at the back of her head.

Tea usually helped her. She was sure that if she drank two cups, she would sleep well enough.

The telephone rang as she was rising from her easy chair to refresh her cup.

"Ginny? It's Rose. Do you have anything that would pass for a maid of honor dress?"

"Excuse me? What . . .?"

"Clayton's asked me to marry him. And I think we need to get that done before he changes his mind. I'm thinking of using my bench in the park. Do you think a minister will do a ceremony where the bride and groom are both sitting? I think my knees are as wobbly as Clayton's now."

Ginny didn't get much sleep that night. But it wasn't because she was fretting. It was because she was so full of joy for Rose and Clayton that she felt like bursting.

She did what she usually did when she felt full of joy. She moved into her workroom and started to design her next art doll. She didn't know what time period or place the doll would represent, but Ginny knew that it would be a wedding doll—and that it would be a wedding present for Rose and Clayton.

Chapter Five

"Don't tell me you've never been to Tybee Island before. And you've lived in Savannah how long?"

"I've been here over ten years," Ginny answered, "and, no, this is my first time out here. I almost came here soon after I arrived in Savannah, but that didn't happen and I never got another offer. I haven't owned a car of my own since moving to Savannah, so I haven't gotten out of the city much."

"Your Lenny never said anything about bringing you out here?" Paul asked.

"No, Lenny isn't much for the ocean. He's very much a city man. He didn't own a car in Savannah either—although he has one in Richmond. He said that sand reminded him of his tour in Iraq." Ginny paused for a minute and looked out into the ocean. When she resumed, her voice had a sad tone to it. "Lenny says he doesn't need any reminders of his time in Iraq, and I'll have to agree with him there."

Even though it had been ten years, Ginny had never forgotten her almost trip to Tybee Island. Tom Thornton was going to bring her out here—her first trip outside Savannah since she had arrived. And this was when Ginny still looked on Tom as a possible love interest. But he got the letter from Edward from a hospital in Washington, D.C., admitting he was deathly ill but telling Tom not to come. And instead of going out to Tybee Island with Tom, Ginny had pushed Tom out into his car to go to Edward.

Ginny had never regretted that decision, but she had often regretted not coming out to Tybee Island. She also didn't regret that now, even after ten years, she still didn't have a car in Savannah. Everything she had needed had been within walking distance of Chatham Square—and she had grown to thinking that everything and everyone she needed was right there on the square.

"Look out there. Can you see it? That's the fake light house at Harbor Town on Hilton Head. I think it's quite amusing that what is perhaps the most photographed lighthouse in the world isn't even a real lighthouse. And there, to the west of that, is Daufuskie Island. Quite an exclusive retreat island for the wealthy. The only way you can get there is by small boat."

"It's such a clear day. I feel like I can see forever. Oops."

"Steady there, Matey," Paul sang out as a blast of wind almost knocked Ginny off her feet. He wrapped an arm around her, pulling her close to the railing at the top of the Tybee lighthouse. When the gust passed them by, he kept her in a tight embrace at his side, and Ginny made no effort to move away from him.

"And I feel like I could stand here, with you, forever," Paul whispered into Ginny's ear.

"And me too," Ginny murmured back. But then she caught herself and laughed and straightened up. This loosened Paul's grip on her and broke the spell of the moment. "But right now I'm famished. And you said there'd be time at the beach afterward, but I don't know . . . I don't have my suit on underneath this."

"No problem. We'll go to MacElwee's for lunch. It's close by on our way out to the resort area. I think you'll love it. Just a ramshackle joint out on the main road, but it serves some of the best beer-battered seafood I've ever had. And then we'll go to the house. It's on 12th Street and is just the second house in from the beach. We can both change there."

"The house?"

"Yes. It's part of the Armstrong Inn holdings now. But my family used to use it a lot. I think you'll find it fits in well with Tybee laid-back style."

"And that's how you know the restaurant too? Because your family used to vacation here?"

"Yes. I've always loved the beach."

"So have I." Saying that surprised Ginny. It was true. She did love the beach. Before Lenny had gone off to Iraq, they'd gone to the beach—either Virginia Beach or Nags Head—whenever they could. Lenny had loved it then too. It was only after he'd returned from the war that they'd stopped going. Now that Ginny thought about it, it seemed like there were a lot of things she'd once enjoyed doing that she stopped doing after Lenny returned from Iraq.

"But how did the inn acquire the house?" she went on to ask, not changing the topic in discussion with Paul but doing everything she could to turn her thoughts away from Lenny at the moment. She felt carefree and adventuresome. She hadn't felt this free and energized for years. And she didn't want to think about Lenny at a time like this.

"It's always been in the family. The inn has been in the family too. Rose Drayton is my great aunt."

"Your great aunt? Rose is your great aunt? So, you came to the Armstrong Inn—?"

"To keep the management of the inn in the family? No, not really, although hotel management was what I trained to do. No, I came to Chatham Square because Aunt Rose told me there was something there that I had to see—that she thought I'd like."

Ginny looked up sharply into Paul's face and saw there exactly what she both feared and hoped to see.

"And she was right. I saw exactly what I wanted in Chatham Square," Paul continued.

Flustered, Ginny looked away, suggesting that they leave the lighthouse and go to lunch. She didn't want Paul to see her blush.

Paul had been right about how delicious the lunch would be—and he also was right about how comfortable and perfectly placed the white-painted, blue-tin-roofed wooden house surrounded on three sides by a deep screened porch

93

was, wedged in the sand within hearing of the Atlantic Ocean surf.

For the next hour, Ginny forgot about Savannah and her concerns there and Richmond, and her fiancé there, as she cavorted with Paul at the edge of the surf and beyond. Exhausted at last, she ran behind him up from the water to where he'd stuck an open beach umbrella in the sand and laid out a large blanket. He threw a towel to her and took one up for himself. He was still standing there, toweling himself off, between her and the ocean, when she'd settled on the blanket and wrapped the towel around her shoulders.

She couldn't help but admire the cut of his athletic body, but she gave a little cry and looked away in embarrassment when she saw that he was looking down at her with a broad smile on his face.

He dropped down on the sand close beside her and put a towel-covered arm around her shoulder. As she had done at the lighthouse railing, she leaned into him rather than away from him and gave a little sigh. This was answered by a sigh of his own.

They sat there, in silence, enjoying watching the activity on the sand and in the surf and the feel of the warm breeze swirling under the canopy of the umbrella.

After what seemed like an eternity, Paul spoke. "You seem to be a million miles away."

"Not so," Ginny answered. "I am here with every fiber of my being. I am totally enjoying this. Thank you for asking me to come out here with you."

"I've been scheming this outing from the moment I first saw you. You are quite pensive, though. A quarter for your thoughts—as I'm sure you realize, it's always more expensive at the beach than at home, so a penny won't do."

Ginny laughed. "Oh, I've had quite a few thoughts running through my mind. I'm totally relaxed."

"OK, how about your darkest thoughts first."

Ginny didn't respond for a moment. There's no way she would tell Paul—or anyone else—what her darkest thoughts were. But she had several dim ones she could choose from. "I was thinking of life at Chatham Square. I've developed such good and quirky friendships there. I think the square idea was a real winner for urban planning. We have a gem of a park to look upon—and to see each other on the square. We don't just coexist in an urban jungle sort of way on the square. We see each other. I mean really see each other. And we appreciate and enjoy each other. And we help each other. That seems to be easier to do in a city sectioned off in distinct small neighborhoods like this. Richmond has similarities to Savannah, but it doesn't have the feel that Savannah has of a collection of small, nearly self-contained micro communities."

"I can sense that this is true," Paul answered in a low voice. "I've only been there a short while, but I already feel like it's home—and that the family sharing the square is an ideal size. But why is this a dark thought?"

"It all seems to be changing. And all at once. Some who were vibrant when I arrived are old and tired and will not, I fear, be there for very much longer. And children—like Samantha and Jeff Turnball—who we all watched grow up, and grew and learned with, are inevitably moving on too. It's all changing. And I don't want it to."

"It's the curse of Savannah, I'm afraid."

"Excuse me?"

"Savannah is one of the hold-out cities of the South. It is somewhat remote in location, and this makes it much more remote in time. It's retained the laziness—but, no, people aren't lazy there—it's retained the sleepiness and slow pace and genteelness of the old South, but that only makes the inevitable passage of time more bittersweet. Because you can't hold back the passage of time, even in Savannah."

"Yes, I think I understand. But when it changes—"

"Ah, but that's the charm of Savannah. When time changes, Savannah just gracefully bends with it, and, although the characters on the stage will change, Chatham Square will retain its unique flavor. And as much as the faces change, the character of the square will remain. I don't know if I'm making any sense at all with that. I'm sorry. I'm probably just making it darker."

"No, thanks. I think that helps. I got a sense of that the other day when the novelist, Helena Jordan, stopped by the table of regulars at the café on the square. She fit in fine with us, and then Tony took her off to where a couple that only recently came to the square was sitting—and they all were getting along just fine too."

They were quiet for several more moments before Ginny spoke again. "But I can't help but regret that it isn't staying the same as I found it. Slow pace and all, which, I can tell you that I noticed—even having come from another southern city, Richmond—and haven't always fully appreciated."

"You know what the Savannah workman told a northern visitor about the pace of his day, don't you?"

"No, I haven't heard that one."

"When asked how his usual day went, he answered in a slow drawl, 'You know, in the morning, when we get up, we like to start off real slow—and then we taper down from there as the day goes on.'"

They shared a comfortable laugh at that.

"And your brightest thought? What would that be?"

Ginny held her breath for a moment, wondering if she would say it—if she could possibly say it. And then she did. "My brightest thought was in wondering if the beds in the house have sheets on them."

Hours later, when Paul had to push the speed limit to get back in time for his four o'clock shift at the Armstrong Inn, he had to let Ginny off in front of her apartment house and leave her with just a peck of a kiss. Ginny didn't mind a bit, as he had given her much more attention than that after they left the beach.

No doubt Ginny would have been mortified to know that anyone had seen even the brief kiss at her apartment door. And, in the event, someone did. Rose was sitting on her bench in the middle of the square and thus had a grandstand seat view of the return of Paul and Ginny. She smiled when she saw the car pull up with the two of them inside, and then she broke out in a grin when she saw her great nephew kiss her good friend. The grin returned to a very self-satisfied smile that held her throughout the evening.

Ginny was humming happily as she mounted the stairs to the second floor of her townhouse apartment building. This was interrupted, however, by the realization that the sound of a TV program from behind her front door was floating out into the hallway. She certainly hadn't remembered leaving the set on. Watching TV wasn't one of her pleasures.

As she turned the key in the door and opened it, she was equally surprised to see that the lights were on in the apartment.

"Hi, babe. I wondered where you were. Just got the urge to run down and surprise you. I've been crazy missing you."

"Lenny!"

* * * *

"What is it, son? What couldn't you have told me over the telephone?"

Jim Turnball entered the basement apartment on Chatham Square and took the small bag of groceries he was carrying directly to the kitchen. He usually came home with a small parcel; it was his share of what they called spoilage at the grocery store—blemished fruits and vegetables, punctured dry goods boxes, and bent cans. What the law allowed of such goods went to area soup kitchens, but the grocery market owners let the employees divvy up the rest. The Turnballs no less than any of the other employees relied on these goods to make ends meet.

"It's not that I couldn't tell you, Dad. It's that I can't figure it out, and I don't want to appear the fool. I need you to look at the letter. It can't mean what I think it means."

"Here, give it to me. Who's it from?"

"The admissions office at Georgia State."

"Oh, god, no, here it comes," Jim thought. "I was afraid of this. Turnballs don't luck out. There's been a mix-up in their offer. This will crush my boy. Oh, god, no, please."

But when he looked at the letter, he initially couldn't believe it meant what it seemed to say either. He read it again and then he pulled out a chair at the table and sat down, and the suspicion of what this meant started to gnaw at him. He'd held it in all these years. He had to hold on now too. He couldn't let Jeff—or anyone else—see how this really affected him, deep down.

"It says you can go to Georgia State for four years, tuition, room, board, and books all paid for—and regardless of whether you make the basketball team or not."

"That's how I read it too. But then I thought there must be some sort of glitch. This doesn't happen. If they even have scholarships like this, why would they give one to me? It can't be my grades for being a scholar or a superman with charity work. I always had real work I had to do."

"I've read it three times now, Jeff. I think it's clear in what it says. But I don't think it's a regular scholarship either. Could you go someplace for a little while—someplace where I know I can find you? I have a couple of phone calls to make."

"Sure, Dad. I'll go out to the square. But should I not tell anyone about it yet? Are you calling to tell them they made a mistake?"

"No, I don't think so. And, yes, go ahead and crow it to the world, if you like. You may not have had the grades or the community work—at least in the way your high school defined it—but I don't think there's any more deserving kid for this than you. And that's why I have to make these calls."

Jeff left the apartment somewhat perplexed on what calls his dad had to make and why he was so serious all at once. He saw that Rose was on her bench, which was where he had originally been headed, but when he veered off to head someplace else, she waved to him and patted the bench beside her.

So, he went over and sat with her. She was working on one of those crazy quilts of hers that seemed such a mess in the process but that turned out so beautiful in the end. Ginny had once said that this was Rose all over—that she looked like she was starting a mess when she got her nose into what was going on in the Chatham Square community but that, in the end, everything turned out beautiful. And there Rose would be, sitting quietly off to the side, smiling a smile of self-satisfaction. And not always telling anyone what part she had in the wonderful thing that happened.

"I haven't seen you since Tuesday, Jeff. Since you delivered the groceries. I hope you've been spending your time wisely."

"Yes, ma'am, thanks. I've tried to. Mr. Winthrop must be feeling a lot better for you to be out here by yourself. If so, I'm glad to know it."

"Yes, he's been downright chipper for days. But I'd still not leave him for very long. Samantha is with him. This is bath day."

"Oh," Jeff said.

"So, maybe you'd like to sit a while and visit with me and then you'd be here when Samantha comes out and tells me it's time for me to go back. She couldn't very well not sit and talk to you for a while then. Our Samantha, as I'm sure know, is much too polite for that."

Jeff blushed and lowered his eyes, and Rose gazed at him benignly with a little self-satisfied look in her eyes.

"I understand you might be leaving us and going to Atlanta—to Georgia State to attend college."

"Yes, ma'am, I might be doing that. I just found out I'm getting full support if I go there."

"That's wonderful news," Rose said, with a smile on her face and a twinkle in her eye. "Hotel management, I hear."

"Yes, ma'am, that's right."

"I think you'd be a wonderful hotel manager. I do hope that you come back and work for us at the inn when you have your degree. Paul has told me how proud he has been with the work you've taken up at the inn now and again. We like to keep

101

family hands involved—and you're as much family to us as anyone else is."

"Yes, ma'am, thanks. I'm sort of hoping that's how it will work out too. I love the square and I'd sure like . . . oh, excuse me, that's my dad walking this way."

Jeff watched his dad approach, the expression on his face inscrutable.

After the usual polite southern exchanges of greetings between Rose and Jim were over, Jeff's dad said, "I hope you'll excuse our rudeness, Ms. Rose, but Jeff and I have to go see someone. So, if you excuse us . . ."

"Oh, don't mind me. It was quite pleasant to have the chance to chat with Jeff. He's always so busy needing to be off somewhere to help someone else when he brings the groceries to the house. And, again, Clayton and I wish to thank you for starting that delivery service up at the grocery store. You've been real neighborly and a life saver for us. I only regret that Jeff has to leave so soon and won't be here when Samantha comes out of the house to relieve me."

She gave another one of her mischievous smiles then, and Jeff blushed and lowered his eyes again, unable to look at either of the adults.

He looked up and registered surprise, though, when his father took his arm and led him off toward the west side of the square and then across the street and up the marble steps leading up to the double doors of Helena Jordan's house.

Jane Seldon answered the door, looking not too pleased. "She's expecting you. She's in the parlor just in here to the right."

As they entered the parlor, Jane withdrew toward the back of the house. Helena was standing, stiffly at the gigantic fireplace, dwarfed by its mantel, her eyes glistening as if ready to cry and her lower lip trembling.

"Hello, Jane," Jim Turnball said in a low voice that showed signs of being on the edge of control.

He had every intention of maintaining that control, though, and not to show any of what he really felt. This was his son. And this was his son's chance to pull himself up into a better life than Jim had been able to give him, although god knew Jim had done the very best for his son that he was able to do. It was very hard to have had to do it alone, though.

"Hello, Jim," Jane answered in a voice with little more control than Jim was able to muster.

Turning to his son, Jim said in a low, husky voice, "Jeff, this is your mother. I've known she was here since she moved in, but we thought it best not to tell you for a while. She's the one who is willing to pay your way to Georgia State. She says she wants to cover your college—that she's quite capable of the expense—and that she wants to be a part of your life now. And I reckon that you should let her do both—it's what she wants, and it's what you both need, I think."

Jim Turnball had been sacrificing for his son Jeff's entire life. He had been resisting letting Jane reveal who she was to his son until now because no matter how stifled she'd

103

felt she was when she left them, and how out of synch with the life she wanted to have, Jim could not come to terms with her desertion. This was why he had taken his son and disappeared into oblivion. But Jim loved his son, and he would make this last sacrifice for him—not only to give him a chance to go to college and better his life but also to not stand in the way of Jeff having a relationship with his mother without all of the added baggage of what had been Jim and Jane's short and turbulent marriage.

* * * *

"Can you sit for a few minutes and chat?" Rose asked Samantha as the young lady came out into the square after attending to Clayton's needs. Dusk was approaching, which was Rose's favorite time of the day on her bench in the square, and she wasn't anxious to leave the park. She also had a couple of things to talk to Samantha about.

"Sorry, I can't, Rose. My mother called and asked me to come on home as soon as I could. Mr. Winthrop seems to be doing so much better this week. Don't you think?"

"Yes. His spirits are up." Just not up far enough, Rose went on to think. "Which leads to something I've wanted to ask you. I won't make you tarry, though."

"Yes?" Samantha asked. She almost sat on the bench, but she remembered in time that she couldn't. It was unusual for her mother to call her like that. If she hadn't already received the letter the day before yesterday, she might have thought that was what this was about. Even though she couldn't stay, she did notice the quilt pieces Rose was working and she did feel she needed to say something to be neighborly. "Those are really nice colors, Rose. I don't think I've ever seen—"

"You haven't seen anyone try to put them together before, have you?" Rose cackled. "I'll let you see it when I've finished, and you can tell me whether it's too garish or not."

"No . . . I'm sure . . . they'll be fine."

"And you are a fine young woman for fibbing to me like that. What I'd like to ask you before you dash off is whether you'll be my bride's maid. Ginny's going to be the maid of honor. There aren't all that many women in this town who'd I'd like to stand with me. I'm going to wear white, and I don't want to hear any sniggering from the sidelines."

"Yes, I'd be pleased to stand with you," Samantha answered. And it was clear from the expression on her face that she'd be very pleased indeed. "So, it's true what Mr. Winthrop said. The two of you are going to be married. No wonder he was so chipper."

"It was that or gas, I suppose," Rose said. And then she laughed.

"It certainly has made you your old self too," Samantha responded.

"Well, I'm sorry about that. I'll try to behave better."

They both laughed.

"Where is the ceremony going to be held?"

105

"I originally was thinking right here, at this bench. But now I think we'll do it by the fountain in Forsyth Park. We can pretend we went to Niagara Falls for our honeymoon. The next day neither Clayton nor I will remember that the gush of water we heard was just a Savannah fountain."

"Over in that park? That seems so—"

"Far away from here—from our own little square? Well, I have my reasons. And I'm saving those for the wedding."

"Who will perform the ceremony?"

"Tony's drumming up someone for us."

"Tony? Our Tony? Our Tony from the female impersonation club downtown?"

"Yes, I thought that would be good for laughs—but never fear, I'll be checking his—or her—credentials for conducting a wedding real careful. Tony so wanted to help, though, and I refuse to put him in a bridesmaid dress. I half fear he'll arrive in a wedding dress that will make me look limp. So, I've given him enough chores around the edges to keep him busy and happy. All I can say is that the Forsyth Park fountain will be better dressed than it ever has been. But, you were needed at home. And here I'm jawing away. Scat, Missy, we'll talk dresses later."

As Samantha was walking away, Rose remembered the other thing she wanted to tell her—who she saw walking up the steps to Samantha's apartment house. "Oh, well, I guess she'll find that on her own."

And find it out on her own Samantha did, although she would have much appreciated the warning. As she climbed the stairs to her third-floor apartment, she heard the noise of conversation and laughter coming down the stairwell from her floor. She opened the door to her apartment to find, sitting at her dining table, because there wasn't enough room for everyone on the living room furniture, not only her parents but William Madison's parents as well. And, sitting pushed a bit away from the table and looking just about as dejected—and angry—as he could get away with under the circumstances hovered William himself.

Samantha blushed immediately. She'd been avoiding William since the drunken night he'd pawed her in the alley behind their houses.

"Well, there she is," Mr. Madison boomed. "And a beauty she is too. We've been wanting to meet you for some time, Samantha, and Billy keeps promising to bring you home to meet us, but he never has managed to do that. Your parents were kind enough to invite us over for dinner."

Samantha looked at the table and saw that it was just the usual Saturday night meal at her house—fried chicken, collard greens, and mashed potatoes. Her first reaction was extreme embarrassment. And then she wanted to kick herself. The Madisons didn't seem put off by the meal her mother had put on the table, so why should she be? That's when she realized that it just wasn't going to be a go with William. She'd been embarrassed because he was—because he was ashamed of her family and the "class" she was from.

"Well screw him," she thought, and smiled and welcomed the senior Madisons to her home—knowing full well that it was probably the last time she'd ever see them, and that it wouldn't be their fault—that they were probably a lovely couple.

Samantha spent the rest of the meal being just as charming as she could be, and the Madisons—not counting William—were comfortable to be charming right back. And both proved to know more about what was going on in the square than had seemed likely. Samantha had always thought they held themselves aloof from life in the square, but she knew now that this had just been William pretending that they were too good for everyone else here.

"I'm glad, but a little surprised that Rose Drayton and Clayton Winthrop are finally getting married," Jasmine Johnson said at one point. "The talk at the inn was that there was something going on between him and that novelist who has moved onto the square and into his house, Helena Jordan."

"I don't think it's that," Mr. Madison interjected as his wife and Jasmine started to delve deeper into that relationship. "I'm Clayton's attorney, and he had me contact Ms. Jordan, but it wasn't about any romantic interest. Clayton had discovered there was someone here in Savannah Helena Jordan had been looking for, and she came here because of that. Can't really say any more about that, but I think it's only been Rose in Clayton's mind for some years now. He just wanted to be in better health before asking her to take him on formally. He told me he didn't want to pin her down when the going got tough. I guess he's doing better."

"Or perhaps it's because he knows he isn't going to get better," Rodney Johnson said in a quiet voice. The two elder couples looked Samantha's way. William was studying a cobweb in the corner of the ceiling and trying to pretend he wasn't even there.

"He's happier now—when he's lucid," Samantha responded in a small voice. "But I don't think he thinks he's getting better, no."

They were all quiet for a few moments.

Mr. Madison broke the stillness with a change of subject. "And you, Samantha. You'll be graduating this year, won't you? Do you have plans, or are you going to stay here and continue being our Florence Nightingale on the square?"

"I think my plans are settled now." Samantha set her gaze on William, without trying to make it obvious that she had. His attention came back to her. There was a brief flash of hopefulness in his eyes, but Samantha made no effort of signaling her reassurance. "I received an acceptance to Georgia State in Atlanta the day before yesterday—with a full scholarship. I hope to go on to Emory's medical school from there. I have my EMT license now, too, so I hope to work with a rescue service while I'm going to school and earn my spending money."

"And Jasmine and I have money to help too," Rodney interjected.

Samantha turned her eyes on her dad and said, "Yes, thanks, that will see me through as well."

109

"Well, well. You're going to make a great doctor," Mr. Madison said, and Samantha thought he said it with genuine admiration.

She would have been flabbergasted to know what he was thinking—which was that she would have no financial problems with college at all. He was Rose Drayton's attorney too. He knew all about the college fund the residents of the square had set up for Samantha and had been feeding for years—even though she wouldn't know about it until she was eighteen.

He was pleased she was going away to college. He admired her even more now, though, because she had worked out a way to a goal herself without knowing that she had a crutch in the fund. She was such a good catch for his son, he thought. If anything, Billy would have to rise to her level to deserve her. His son would be a fool not to snatch her up.

William's look at Samantha told a different story, however. By going away to college, she was giving him a "no" answer. By going to Georgia State—where Jeff Turnball also was going—she was telling him so much more. And William only half understood why she was turning him down like this. He could only remember snatches of what had happened in that alley while he'd been in a drunken stupor—and she'd finally gotten what she wanted, didn't she? To meet his parents. Although, he didn't think that had worked out any better than he had imagined it would. It certainly wasn't working well for him.

* * * *

"What is it, child? You were whispering on the telephone and sounded distraught."

"Oh, Rose. I just don't know what to do."

It was late in the evening, and Rose had opened her front door to Ginny and motioned her toward the kitchen at the back of the house. She had already put the tea kettle on. She thought she knew what Ginny wanted to talk to her about. But she was wrong, and she was sad in being wrong.

"It's Lenny," Ginny said as soon as she settled in a kitchen chair.

"What's Lenny?"

"He's back. He's lying on my sofa and snoring up a storm."

"Drunk?"

"No. Just exhausted. He said he drove straight through from Richmond. Said he couldn't wait to see me again. He had such a boyish way about him. I could almost see a wagging tail."

"And that's what has you unsettled?"

"Yes."

"Oh, child. I can give you tea and comfort. But I'm the last one in the world to give you any sort of advice. Look at what I've gone through—what Clayton and I have put each other through. I could tell you to go with your heart, but look at the mess I made out of dithering around with that myself."

"I'll . . . I'll take the tea and comfort now and be glad of that. It's my dilemma and I guess I'll work it out. But why does everything have to change now? I . . . we all were going along so well."

"It's Savannah time, honey. It lulls us into thoughts that nothing's going to change—that nothing needs to change. But time goes on regardless. And it's a good thing it does. We'd be in a hell of a rut if it didn't."

"That's what Paul told me today. He got the concept of Savannah time from you, didn't he? You were naughty not to tell me he was your great nephew."

"Ah, Paul. Does any of this have anything to do with Paul?"

"Yes, I think so . . . oh, I don't know."

"It'll come to you, Ginny. You have a good head on your shoulders. You'll figure it out."

Rose lowered her head and sipped her tea so that Ginny couldn't see her Cheshire Cat expression.

Chapter Six

It was quite a fun joke that Tony played on the wedding party the afternoon Rose and Clayton got married in front of the central fountain in Forsyth Park, the huge urban green zone that marked the boundary between Savannah's glorious historical district and it's not-so-manicured new city. Rose reveled in the joke.

Tony had found a woman minister who looked just questionable enough in gender for all of the guests to entertain themselves with guessing games. While the guests happily buzzed, the wedding party, sans Tom and Edward, who Rose vaguely thought would join them in the van—but a point Rose was hazy on when the scheduled departure time had come and gone—arrived at the park. They were bundled out of the Armstrong Inn van and processed en masse to the arched frame by the fountain that Tony had also fashioned, complete with white muslin drapes, with just one panel of bright scarlet "for effect," he said, while he muttered "and for truth in packaging" in sotto voce.

Flanking Rose, dressed, as she threatened, in a white cotton muumuu, but still looking remarkably good for her age, were Clayton in a wheel chair being wheeled by Paul, on the one side, and Arnie Richards, in another wheel chair being steered by Tony, on the other side. Arnie had accepted the chore of giving Rose away with delight—even after she quite pointedly established that no one gave Rose away—that it was all just symbolic. Arnie had retorted that what was symbolic was that he represented all of the folks living on Chatham Square, who were the ones who weren't, by any means, giving either Rose or Clayton away.

Ginny and Samantha, both dressed in blue summer smocks, trailed behind.

It was Tony who grabbed the attention of those who were sitting in front of the arch on folding chairs and redirected them from speculation on the origin of the minister when the wedding party sauntered in. Dressed to the nines in a black tuxedo, frilly white shirt, and quite conspicuous red cabbage rose in his lapel, with make-up that must have been applied with a trowel, on this day Tony was playing as a man parading as a woman in a man's tuxedo.

Once more shocking and delighting everyone in attendance, the minister Tony had commissioned broke out in a la-la-ing of the traditional wedding processional—in a quite convincing and rich contralto—or was that a tenor?

Before the wedding party got into position, Rose stopped and announced to everyone, "Sorry we're late, folks. Tom didn't make the bus. He's supposed to be Samantha's attendant. We thought we'd gotten the plans mixed up and that he and Edward would already be here—but I see they're not here yet."

"You did remember to tell them about the wedding, didn't you?" Clayton sang out.

"Well, now that you mention it . . ." Rose answered, with a dubious expression on her face, and in a voice that trailed off into a mutter. "We'll give them a few minutes and then they can just enjoy the photographs if they aren't here in time. Someone did bring a camera, didn't they?"

Everyone looked around expectantly, but then the minister reached into a hidden pocket in her voluminous ministerial garb and came up with a camera that she handed off to Jeff Turnball.

And then, breaking all tradition, which she undoubtedly delighted in doing, Rose left the rest of the wedding part to take up their positions while she, herself, went among the seated guests and greeted them. She stopped in front of Jeff, who was seated between his father, Jim, and his mother, Helena—with a scowling Jane Seldon on the other side of Helena possessively holding onto her arm—and batted her eyes and said, "Glad you and your parents could make it. Have you heard? Samantha's going to be going to Georgia State in the fall, just like you. Isn't that spiffy?" She winked at Jim as she passed by, and he gave her a grateful smile back.

Jeff looked surprised and then grinned from ear to ear and turned his eyes on Samantha. Samantha was looking at where her parents sat with the Madisons, the four of them

115

chatting away comfortably, and said a little prayer that the two couples would remain friends even after they learned there would be nothing to be had in a pairing of her and William. Her parents needed friends—especially after she went away to college. Knowing that the center of their lives would be missing when she was gone had been a major impediment to her deciding to go away to college. Until now they both had spent all of their time working to give her a life and a future.

William, of course, hadn't deigned to attend the wedding, although he'd been invited.

Feeling eyes boring into her, Samantha did turn and look at Jeff in time to see his big grin, though, and she smiled back. She felt she wouldn't regret her decision, even though it wasn't a fairytale ending by any means. Being coupled with Jeff would be fraught with its own problems. Samantha was much too sensible not to realize that.

At last Rose returned to the tableau set before the minister, robed in white, who was being as patient and pleasant as she possibly could be, and they remained there for a few minutes, everyone focused on the empty spot beside Paul, functioning as the best man, where Tom should be standing.

As they waited, Rose, leaned into Ginny and murmured, "You can stop carrying around that brochure on Forsyth House now that Arnie gave you to try to pawn off on me. I know it's been burning a hole in your purse and consciousness."

"What?" Ginny responded in surprise. She blushed like a toddler with its hand caught in the cookie jar.

"I know Arnie charged you to talk to Clayton and me about going into a nursing home. Clayton was ahead of him on that. He's arranged for us to go into Forsyth House—just a few days behind Arnie. That's why we're having the wedding here, just across the road from the place. We'll tell everyone at the end of the ceremony that there's no reason they can't visit us there, because they were all able to find their way this far today."

"Oh."

"Don't look so dejected. Arnie told me he pointed out to you that it's just a couple of blocks from Chatham Square, so it's not like we are leaving the community. And may I surmise that you aren't leaving the community either?"

"What do you mean?"

"I saw your Lenny lugging his suitcase back down the stairs of your apartment house this morning. Does that mean you've sent him back to Richmond empty nested?"

"God, Rose, you see everything, don't you?"

"Yep. Always have—and always will. Don't you forget that, Missy. Well, have we seen the tail end of Lenny?"

"Maybe. It looks like it."

"Good. That fits my plans well. I'm giving the house on the square to SCAD with the proviso that they put your department in it. The master bedroom will be perfect for your workroom. It's got natural light on three sides. And that will free up your second bedroom for when your and Paul's first child comes along."

"Rose!" Ginny exclaimed, blushing with shock.

117

But before Ginny could say anything else, Rose raised her voice and announced to all assembled, "I guess we need to get on with this. Tom and Edward can enjoy it in the photographs. And let's make this snappy. The cake's at the house, but you'll need to cut it and run. Clayton needs his meds and to be back in bed in twenty minutes tops."

Not rattled at all, the minister flipped through the ceremony like an auctioneer. She had just finished the binding part when they heard the sirens. As the sound of the squealing came closer, from the north, and then stabilized just a few blocks away, Rose turned to her maid of honor and bridesmaid and said, "Maybe it's Edward. You two best go. Samantha may be needed. I'll have Paul take you in the van while we're kissy facing here. We'll herd the rest to the house and stuff them with cake until you can report."

"Rose, you might be winding down physically and you may have your lapses from time to time," Ginny thought. "But when you're on, you are still sharp as a tack."

It was, indeed, Edward. But it also was Tom. When Ginny and Samantha got to the bookstore, where paramedics were already working on both men, they were told that Edward had fallen down the stairs and, as Tom was calling 911, he'd had a heart attack. Samantha waded right into the fray, informing those working on both men what the medical histories of the two were, which helped greatly in getting the two stabilized and into ambulances.

Hours later, when the momentous events on the square had settled down, Paul took Ginny to the William's Café for a coffee and so that both could enjoy the twilight and catch their breaths. As they sat there, the two new residents of the square Ginny had seen seated with Tony and Helena on her last visit here—which now seemed eons ago—met casually in front of the café, walking there from different directions; spoke briefly; and then came in and sat at one of the tables and ordered coffee. Ginny had to wrack her brain to remember that the young lady was a teacher and the young man a real estate broker.

"Quite a day," Paul murmured as he was spooning sugar and cream into his coffee.

"Yes, you certainly can't say that we were on Savannah time today," Ginny responded. "Every minute seemed like an hour, certainly, but every hour brought change crashing down on us here in Chatham Square."

"Have you heard from the hospital yet?"

"Samantha's called me a few times from there. It's still touch and go on both of them. One thing is for sure, though. They won't be able to come back to the bookshop. Those stairs up to the second floor are just too steep and long. That young lady is a treasure. She's stuck with Tom and Edward every step of the way. I'll be going back this evening to relieve her and force her to go home. Jeff's with her there, though, so she has company and support."

"Do you think the two of them—?"

"Who can tell? They both are just starting out in life. Leaving the square for college will inevitably bring new directions in their lives—even though they're going to the same college. I certainly wouldn't mind if they both came back as a couple to live with us here again."

"With us here again? Does that mean you've decided to stay in Chatham Square?"

"What, Rose didn't tell you? She's slipping. Yes, I think I'll sign on at the college for at least another year. With Edward out, the department doesn't need to be challenged by more change."

"Ah, that ever-threatening change."

"Yes, well. As both you and Rose said, it's going to happen. But we should try to make the best of it."

They sat there in silence for a few moments, and when the silence was broken again, it was Ginny who spoke. "And speaking of change that doesn't change the character of the square, just the characters themselves, I think it's time that I met those two at the other table—the beginning of the next generation on the square. You with me?"

Ginny rose, as did Paul, and both moved across the café.

"Hello, I'm Ginny Standler and this is Paul Prentice. I believe you're our newest residents on the square. I think it's time we welcomed you to the community."

Sue Staples, the teacher, and Grayson Hendricks, the real estate broker, looked up from their coffees, both smiling, both happy to become more deeply embedded in the life of Chatham Square.

Olivia Stowe

Olivia Stowe is a published author under different names and in other dimensions of fiction and nonfiction and lives quietly in a university town with an indulgent spouse and one demanding Siamese cat. Olivia is still mourning the loss of her other Siamese, which died suddenly after a short illness.

Books By Olivia Stowe

Charlotte Diamond Mysteries

By the Howling

Retired With Prejudice

Coast to Coast

An Inconvenient Death

Savannah Series

Chatham Square

Savannah Time

Other books

Fiddler's Rest

Spirit of Christmas

www.ingramcontent.com/pod-product-compliance
Lightning Source LLC
Chambersburg PA
CBHW071626140626
46555CB00021B/863